Curtis looked dow
the balcony above
wanted was nowher
people. They swaye
trance to a beat he
thick scent of hashish ... from a spliff between his fingers and he took another pull allowing the image beyond the glass to glow even more to his eyes. Something was to be announced this evening when Carl got here, but nobody knew when he would arrive.

BACKSTREETS

Also in the BACKSTREETS series

BIG UP!

BACKSTREETS

SLACKNESS

JONATHAN BROOK

BOXTREE

First published in the UK in 1994 by
Boxtree Limited
Broadwall House
21 Broadwall
London SE1 9PL

10 9 8 7 6 5 4 3 2 1

Cover Art—Faisal/M. Bishop
Cover Design—Martin Lovelock
Series Editor—Jake Lingwood
Series Production—Joya Bart-Plange

Printed and bound in Great Britain by
Cox and Wyman Ltd, Reading, Berkshire

ISBN: 0 7522 0920 5

A CIP catalogue entry for this book is available from the British Library

Thanks to R.T.

One

He passed by Bliss but the only girls in there were ugly or going out with bulls and he was in no mood for mixing it today. Better to wait for the evening when he could stroll at his leisure through the divine temptations of lone femininity on the dancefloor, flashing his teeth like a beacon.

"So gal, y'alright?"

Flesh was his calling at the moment and the delights of friction filled his thoughts.

Ben was charged already and it was only late afternoon. He normally delayed smoking till later, when he was settled somewhere for the evening, but today he had lit up as soon as he woke. The dull blanket of cloud visible through his window had been enough to drive him to it—so he produced his own nebula, floating against the ceiling of his room. Smoke was his balm against the weeks of miserable weather that had gripped West Park. That and the pursuit of permissive females were his main activities and he usually found this an effective way of preventing the cold touch of reality from sneaking up on him. Ben was quite content to drift for a while.

When he had heard the front door slam he'd known it was time to get up. It gave him a strange feeling of pleasure to visualize the tired frame of his father slumping to the kitchen whilst he had lain in bed for the last few hours and had still to eat breakfast. Now he could dress and prepare to go out before the customary tirade—*So what? You been in bed all day again, then?* If he was careful he could get out to the street without being heard, but if he was caught there would be some task or duty to perform.

Today a creak of the stairs had been enough to seal his fate and he'd been dispatched with a grocery list, but the thought of the market appealed anyhow. When he was charged, the market came to life with noise and colour. Besides, he had the rest of the day to kill.

Ben was conscious of the way he looked and would check his reflection from time to time in a shop front, or car window even. He particularly enjoyed passing electrical shops, as they often had a camera trained on the shoppers marching past and he'd become expert at finding the display monitor, hidden amongst the racks of screens.

In an attempt to combat the monochrome dullness of the day, and under the influence of the chemical floating around his brain, he had chosen the brightest clothes in his wardrobe. The range was limited as Ben had nowhere near enough money to equip himself in the way he would have liked, but he was far from scruffy. His jeans were only a few weeks old and hung just the way he liked them to. They were loose fitting and as he strolled along the denim wrapped around his legs in folds of blue. They almost scraped the street, but the orange and purple logo of his trainers flashed out every few steps. Ben never wore any other kind of footwear. That was the Curtis deal when you started wearing office shoes. He couldn't relax in them—M*e stick to the crepes boy. You wan' feel ya go to a job interview all the time*?

Some of his friends were getting into suits, but Ben made out that it was square. He was too poor to buy any himself, even if he had liked the look. His own jacket was a thin cotton, heavily padded, in the brightest yellow with black lettering on the back. It was a team from the States, not that Ben had any interest in sport, which he found tiring just to watch. The jacket was a straight zip-up, but today it was wide open and the bright reds and greens of his shirt burst out in glorious technicolour.

He knew he looked good, but still he had to check everything was just right whenever he got the chance. Bliss was handy for this as a long mirror ran the length of the bar, enabling him to examine himself whilst scouting for potential victims of the pounce—*You look lonely there gal. I jus' sit down and cheer you right up.*

There was nothing to interest him downstairs, so he stepped past the tables at his easy pace, his body swaying slightly. The coffee drinkers looked up at him as he nosed round the end of the bar and came back, finding nothing.

"Having a drink or just passing by?"

It was a girl talking from behind the bar, dressed in a white blouse that indicated she was staff, but he had never seen her here before. He moved up to the line of stools running the edge and leaned right over so his elbows rested on the gleaming top. Ben was tall and could look over to see she was wearing leggings.

"Well I look for a friend, but him not here. You new, I think?"

"Yes, you think right." She was fiddling with some glasses and he watched her intently for a few seconds.

What was it with women at the moment? His hormones were screaming. Every movement she made was smooth and sensual, even washing a glass. Sometimes lately, Ben would be on the high street, deep in thought, and then would look up at the packed street only to see all the women naked—all with perfect bodies. The fantasy would run rampant through his brain for a few seconds and then slowly vanish. He was obviously not having enough sex for his age, that was the problem.

She turned back to him and noticed his stare. "Yes?"

"Oh nothing." He realised that he was now on the stool, slumped across the bar, an amorous grin fixed across his face. He sat up, not wanting to look dopey, and shot himself a look at the mirror behind her. Surely she liked what she saw?

His face was thin and strong with no hint of fat. The jaw he considered noble, but most people would have said the line was prominent, making him look slightly aggressive. His eyes were fiery with a hint of amber and this added to the vague malevolence of his regard—though Ben was not at all vicious, quite the opposite. He did exploit the hardness of his look though. It would excite some girls to think of him as a man of mystery, and a harsh stare had persuaded many a man not to mess with him.

For a moment he lingered, staring at the mirror. The brown shades and soft lighting of Bliss forming the perfect background.

"Sure you don't want a drink?"

She had broken in on his reverie and he pulled himself back off the stool "Nah, I see you in the evening maybe."

He cruised off, making for the heavy glass entrance door, but there was a shout behind him, disturbing the cinematic coolness of his departure.

"Your groceries are they?"

Escape to the high street. The pavement was a shifting mass of people trying to grab what they needed and then rush off home. He preferred to take it easy and not join the mad rush. Even in West Park you couldn't escape the traffic round this time of day. The street was solid with crawling vehicles, and rather than hop the bus he decided to pace back home in his own time. It would be quicker than public transport anyway.

West Park had the high street winding down past a small park and over to the next borough with the usual range of housing, shops and people you found over this side of town. Bliss was the best bar. The other drinking-holes were a bit downgrade for his liking, with stained carpets and crumbling furniture. You could get hassled in a few of them being black as well.

As the road got closer to the turn for his home, the shops thinned out and were replaced by blocks of terraces and industrial units for a stretch. The ones that remained were fast food dives or scruffy off-licenses, many open long past midnight. Here you could usually step off the main road and find groups of youth selling bits of draw or just hanging out, but the weather was bad so the streets were almost dead. He felt no apprehension about that scene, he was part of it, but Mike complained from time to time if he got a push or a bad word. That was usually later in the night though.

He cut off the high road and took a few turns. The street thinned and he was in the maze where he lived. Cars were parked on both sides, a few of them wrecks just left to rot. Some of the houses were empty, bearing the scars of years of neglect—boards nailed across the doors and windows to stop kids or drunks entering. The odd, tired hound would limp past, pausing at each corner.

Ben didn't notice the run down aspects of his yard. He knew it as a lively place, full of life and energy. This was where he had grown up and embraced the adventure of adolescence. The thought of moving was far from his mind.

One last turn and he was on his street. The grocery bag was getting heavy now and he was relieved to be back. He walked over to the opposite pavement and through the wooden gate to his porch. His father had gone out and there was no response to his knock, so he fumbled for his key and opened the door.

Back in the kitchen he looked up from the table and saw his outline in the window. It was dark now but the bulb above him lit the glass like a mirror and he smiled at himself—*You look criss you know?*

He was admiring the side of his head. A few days before he'd had a pattern cut into his hair—a jagged set of half triangles. He had to stoop to admire himself. Ben was tall and light framed and very happy with it.

After packing the shopping he returned to his room and flopped down on the bed he hadn't left so long ago. The walk had knackered him. It wasn't a good idea to smoke on top of exercise in his opinion, and he decided to have a nap before going out to the club. With the aid of another smoke of course.

He flicked the radio on and lay back, rolling a lazy joint on his chest. All the relevant materials were within his reach at the side of the bed, to accommodate hassle-free rolling. Sticking the papers together, he opened the contents of a cigarette onto them and heated the black on the end of a badge pin. Bearing in mind his imminent voyage to unconsciousness and the huge lump he had come to have in his possession, he crumbled a generous line of black along the ridge of tobacco. In no time the spliff was rolled, sealed, and lit. It was strong and he had to lay it down after a few minutes, then rolled over and fell into sleep.

Ben flicked his eyes open. A second ago he had been in a log cabin somewhere, gradually tearing back the velcro fastening of a ski suit. The blue fabric was a film it was so thin, and so tightly adhered to the body of his partner. She stared at him with fright—wide blue eyes and a trembling rose lip. They lay in bundles of soft hay, sheltering from the elements.

But now something else was on his mind. There was a metallic clicking at his feet and he threw the covers off his bed, sitting up and rubbing his face. The phone was lying there, screaming at him.

"Yes, you have Ben's attention. So, what you say to me then?" He was sure it was Mike. He seemed to have the ability to disturb the fondest moment with an ill-timed call, usually just to chat.

"This C. You going Maxine's tonight?"

The voice surprised him. It had been a while. "Well, I see you is full of casual interest in saying hello and such. Yes, I go there. How is you man?"

"Safe B. So you wanna ride with me?"

"Yeah, course."

"We should have a drink an' that, you know. Don't want to lose touch."

"No, course not."

"So, come now."

"Yeah, give me ten minutes to get change. You coming now anyway, yeah?"

"Ben, go to the window an' lift the curtain a bit."

"Uh?"

"Jus' do it, man."

Ben hopped off the bed, trying to ignore the wash of the drug which had been dormant in his still body. Carrying the phone with him, he walked over to his window and drew back the thick cloth to scan the street.

Curtis was sitting outside in his car. The big black beast he drove was ticking over and Ben could hear the purr of the engine bouncing off the walls of his street. The glass was tinted black, but he had his window down and Ben stared at him for a second before lifting his arm to wave. Curtis was in his ear.

"See me have a mobile now!"

"Me come down as me is then."

He rang off and started rushing about the room. This was good. There had been enough walking today already. Just as he was ready to leave he stopped at the door and thought warmly of his dream, broken by the call. He grinned to himself at Curtis's last words. *Flash bastard these days old* Curtis.

Two

Ben started feeling uneasy about the whole thing as soon as they reached the bridge. Its dirty metal frame towered above him, throwing shadow lines across the car and blocking out the little light that still remained. The day was ending with a surge of wind that sent litter and clouds of gritty dust up into the faces of the pedestrians tramping back from work. They filled both pavements. Faces were hidden by dull scarves and the collars of overcoats. Their clothes were the same tone as the sky, winter's angry dark. He pushed himself back into the warm leather of his seat and reflected on their lives. The crammed dash home to a laboured meal with a bored partner, then sleep and the nightmare of repetition in the morning. That was one way to live he knew he would never choose. He let the music from the speakers buried in the rear dash pulse around his head and stared out through the tinted glass.

The bridge crossed a grey Thames and on either bank there were rows of broken buildings. Industry's relics stretched off to the east. Through the flickering rails of the bridge he could see the brick blocks follow the bend of the river. He felt a rush of nerves as Curtis pulled off the bridge's straight span and took a right, confirming their destination. Rippuh country, it was known as by his friends in the patch, but he thought more of its present menace than the Victorian one and disliked coming here. If Curtis had mentioned where exactly they were going then he would have declined the lift. These days Curtis seemed to talk less and less about where he went or who he went there with. Ben never asked. He had just been happy for a ride to the club.

"Me have a little business to deal with first, if you don't mind B."

He'd assumed they might be picking up a girl or a draw, but what were they doing over here? This could only be some major event to bring Curtis over the river. He hated it as much as Ben. The urge to ask was powerful but he held back. He wanted Curtis to know that he was scared of nothing as there were rumours that his friend was becoming a big man in the yard, may be soon if he kept up his respect. Not that Ben had any such ambitions. He had known Curtis for years and didn't want his friend to believe they were growing apart. A sign of fear would have been enough to persuade him that next time it might be best not to drop by when he had something to do. Ben wanted no obstacles in the course of their friendship. He valued it. Curtis would go a long way to help him out of a problem. He would sit it out.

The streets were already taking on the decrepit look he expected of this part of town. Battered terraces and corner bars were hidden amongst crumbling warehouses. The buildings were low but packed in tightly with each other, so there was no view of the sky and the oncoming night. The street-lamps had come on and the orange glow of trapped gas gave the landscape a surreal edge. Somehow, the false light made it harder to focus on the chipped flagstones and the weekday debris that bordered the road. He was in a blur of broken streets, market stands and glimpses of light from curtained living rooms. There was nobody on the road. The familiar sense of desolation that this end of town gave him was growing stronger as they pressed on and he was aware that he would have great difficulty finding his way out of this mess of tiny streets.

"A we dis Ben."

The car was moving at walking pace down a thin cobbled lane. Sweeping under a railway arch and through high, steel gates they pulled into a yard. He could see brick walls with twisted wire and shards of glass embedded in cement along the top. They made up three sides and the railway bridge made the square. It was not a big enclosure. Ben guessed it was perhaps used as a lock-up or to store equipment as there was a pile of metal in one corner and the cracked asphalt floor was covered in pools of inky liquid, oil or petrol. They parked and Curtis killed the engine. It was so quiet Ben could hear the ticking as it cooled.

After only a few seconds the wash of a high-beam flooded the yard and a car bonnet inched past the gates, stopping halfway through. Ben was scared now. The intent was clear enough. They were going nowhere until things had been concluded. He turned to speak with Curtis, to try and find out what was going to happen, but Curtis was already reaching for the door handle.

"You wid me on dis B? Come now. You have nothin' to do but watch, my friend."

He was out of the door. Ben hesitated for a moment but seeing his friend's back through the windscreen, moving towards the other car, he sighed and got out.

They were only twenty feet or so from the new arrival, standing side by side. Curtis stood tall. He was a year older than Ben but could have passed for more. The last six months had seen a change in him, as though he had aged in years and wisdom. No longer did he wear the light, coloured jackets and jeans that his friends chose. He had a long, leather coat wrapped around his frame and black cord trousers that looked fresh from the bag. Moving with an older gang, he had swapped his crepes for mint brogues. Everything he wore was new. Ben felt childish in comparison. Curtis had a look of maturity in contrast to Ben's casual dress. Not to say that his clothes were cheap. They came for less than they would in a shop though. He could put an order in with the right person. His trainers alone should have been a hundred. He had paid twenty. Ben was well used to cutting corners to get the things he needed. Making your own breaks happen for you was the key, but nothing too serious.

They heard the doors of the other car open and some heavy footsteps. Three men turned around the gates and walked slowly up to them. One man stood at the front, the other two flanking him, so they formed a triangle. Ben saw straight away that they were older than his seventeen years. The lead man must have been in his thirties. He more than matched Curtis in his dress. In the growing dark it was hard to make out details, but Ben could see the expensive cut of his suit and a thin tie. His head was shaved. The two behind him were the escort, thickset and tall, dressed in tacky suede jackets and jeans.

"You know, I'm most surprised that you're here, Curtis."

The voice was thin and educated, not the ugly drawl he had expected. Ben had assumed the man would be local, but the hint of sophistication meant he was from an entirely different walk of life. This disturbed him. The voice had a roll to it, almost theatrical. At least with the cockney tongue you could place your speaker and know how to react.

"Surely you imagined that I would punish you."

The man lingered over the words, gaining pleasure from the menace.

"Zack, I thought we come to talk, that all." The response was assured. Curtis was evidently not afraid of this man.

"You are a child Curtis. If you had any brains you would never have tried to market my territory. I leave you people the other side but you get greedy and start—"

"It get too busy down there. An don't forget I am part of a team, not some fool pickney."

The two stared at one another. The exchange had been rushed and now the man waited a moment in thought. Ben felt like a jumpy spectator, but kept his body tense and head up to show his arrogance. Many times this look had been enough to gain respect and prevent violence.

"You listen to my words Curtis. I was friends with your boss once, you know. He sent you here knowing exactly what I would do. Maybe you should bear that in mind. He obviously wants you humbled—so I will oblige." He raised an arm and motioned to the two behind him. They stepped forward as one.

Ben felt his nerves awaken. He'd had various battles with youth his own age but this was a new level to him. His fights had no criminal element. He knew that these men did this as a way of life. Their faces were impassive, as though set in stone. How could Curtis involve him in this? To back a friend when you were told in advance and when it was over some score to settle was different. Curtis shouldn't have taken him into this situation. In the seconds the two men slowly approached and the front man drifted back towards the car, his heart began to race. This had been a tense encounter so far, one which he later may have laughed over and been proud of backing up a friend, but he wanted no part in a beating.

Meanwhile, Curtis had spent no time pondering the situation. He pulled at his coat and fumbled with the lining, his practised fingers found what they sought and he spun round towards the attackers. They were both moving slowly, lumbering, expecting no problem with slapping some kids around then taking a few notes off the guy in the car. They saw Curtis spin, saw a flash of light behind him, and a line like a stretch of rope. It lifted high into the air, carried by his turn, and made a whistle as it formed an arc.

"Fucker's got a chain!" Their eyes became full of boyish fear and turned up at the bike chain as it swung towards them. There was no time to duck or raise an arm. The hiss of steel on flesh sang out, and the man nearest Curtis raised his hands to his cheek. It was split from eye to jaw. The thick, fleshy edges of the wound gushed blood like a black stain in the dark.

Curtis had lifted his whole body for the swing, uncoiling the chain from the waist of his coat as he sprang. He landed on his feet, crouching low, and jerked it back with a flick of his wrist.

Ben was frozen.

He saw the startled pain of the cut man as he sank to his knees, cursing and trying to stem the flow of blood. Already his clothes were sodden with it. Ben tried to move but couldn't decide what to do. The other man was rushing at Curtis with fury, in a race against him striking out again with the bike chain. The man had been surprised by the attack but not to the point where he couldn't act. His friend was in a mess but it could still be avenged. He was no stranger to the unexpected in a fight.

He was on Curtis as Ben blinked. With the broad hard back of his hand he slapped him in the face, startling him. Curtis was stunned by the blow and dropped his weapon. The man kicked it to one side and lifting his foot, kicked him in the side of the leg, just above the knee. Curtis was crippled by the pain and crumpled to the ground. The man stepped back and glanced over him. He reached down and grabbed Curtis by the hair, yanking his head back to expose his throat.

"Come tooled on me fucker, you pay for it."

He lifted a fist above him and arched his second finger to make a sharp point ready to send it crashing into the soft exposed throat, but Curtis kept a hard-eyed stare and whispered, "Ben . . ."

He had seen the man kick Curtis to the ground and prepare to strike him. Even then he could not act. He'd fallen back to the bonnet of the car and rested against it, panting. The clinical professionalism of the violence was new to him. It was controlled and far removed from the frenzied blows of a youth fight. He knew the oncoming punch could maim his friend and tried to find courage, but wanted to sob. It was only when he heard the muttered plea for salvation that he knew what to do.

Suddenly his body was filled with movement as he rushed at the man leaning over Curtis. With one leap he was in the air and came crashing down into the man's back, his knee catching him at the base of the spine. The man fell sideways and rolled in the grease and dirt of the yard's floor. Ben followed him, giving savage kicks to his head and chest. The feeble defence of the man's raised arms were nothing to the onslaught. Ben was overcome with a blind energy and targeted the man's head until he lay in a pathetic heap, face distorted in pain. Even then he kept kicking until finally the strength ran from his legs. Hardly able to stand, his head spinning and having to breathe deep gulps of air to fill his empty lungs, he began to think again. His victim was finished so he turned to check on Curtis, but saw his friend stumbling off to the car parked in the entrance. He wanted Zack.

In obvious pain Curtis slumped round the gate to the back of the car where Zack reclined, idly waiting for the return of his hired help. Curtis banged his face up to the cold glass of the window and stared in at him. Before the frightened boss could act, he pulled the door open and thrust an arm in to grab at his suit lapel. Curtis broke through the protest of flailing arms and dragged him out, lying on his belly. Zack turned his head to appeal for mercy but was thrown to the floor and pushed against the side of the car before he could speak. Now he knew there was no chance of escaping the aggression and he dropped his eyes in acceptance.

In a frozen second Curtis hesitated, perplexed by the man's surrender, but then drew back an arm and shot five or six quick punches to the side of his head. The blows made a dull thud and by the third one the skin tore and a stream of blood ran down the man's throat, soaking his shirt.

"Fuck with me and I'll mess you up bad boy. I tell my man you send regards, an' that you happy, right?"

There was no reply. Curtis lifted himself up and

walked back to Ben. The pain in his leg was going, the victory bringing a rush of adrenalin into his blood, chasing away the hurt. "Y'all OK Ben? You pull me out when I need it. Me not forget."

Ben was flush with triumph. The violence had charged him up and he was breathing heavily, his body trembling slightly. They stood for a few moments watching the groaning shapes of the vanquished, then Curtis moved back across to the other car. Stopping at the back he nudged Zack with his foot so that the unconscious man fell away.

"Don't want to be too cruel to Zachariah."

He chuckled and climbed into the driver's seat then let the hand-brake off and kicked back with his foot on the ground. The car began to roll back slowly, clearing the gates for their exit, and he hopped out of the seat before it picked up speed. The car freewheeled a few yards until stopping on the far kerb. Ben had watched the action in silence. The calm of the night and the isolated location meant he could hear the soft stroke of the tires on the asphalt. He was still full of nervous energy but a numbing relief was washing over him and he longed for the cruise back to the club. Surrounded by a wall of sound in the car he could play back the memory of his charge over and over, and relish the way he knew Curtis would describe their battle to his partners in the gang. "Come on then, Curtis. Me thirsty you know. You drag me out here for this without me even having a drink."

"Soon come B. We go down Maxine's, yeah?"

Three

Maxine's was busy for a weekday. As they pushed past the suited doorman and muttered greetings, they could smell the sweat and heat from the dance room. Instead of walking through to the main room though, they turned and climbed a thin staircase to the upper bar. The beat of the music was still a loud rumble here, but people could talk. This was where Curtis had first met the man he worked for, where he took his orders and reported in. At first he'd wanted to move alone. Since he was sixteen he had taken risks and gradually progressed to building a fair name for himself round the patch. Gangs kept you working for others and there was no real loyalty. Everyone wanted to be the man and it was hard to run things smoothly. Curtis liked being chief and had got by fine selling bits of draw and setting up his friends to do the same. From this stage he began to look for a more profitable trade, maybe crack to a chain of dealers. He knew how the money could roll in and he thought nothing of the risks. That was the run of the game. A man should live his time fast, take what he wants and show he fears no other. That was his creed.

Curtis was eighteen now. He wanted money by his twenties. Money was the key. Carl was helping him to find it. Shifting from weed to powder meant having contacts, capital and respect. His attempts to break through on his own had failed and left him confused. From hanging at Maxine's he had seen the dealings going on and heard talk that this man Carl was a player. Curtis was London born and knew it was a disadvantage. The boys from J had the rep. He wanted a chance though, and badly. So he confronted Carl at his corner table one night and the show of face secured him some small respect. Curtis was given the job.

That was three months ago and things had been going well. The second week he was given the car. Weekly hand-outs allowed him to dress up the way he wanted and immediately he started to separate from Ben and the others. It was a weakness to be seen with people outside the circle anyway. He wanted no chink in his reputation. But it was hard to cut out Ben. They went back a long way. However, such was his drive to cut through the ranks and eventually break out on his own he could make sacrifices.

They were standing at the bar now. Ben was still beaming from the fight, eager for applause, but Curtis was cool. He had things to dwell on. The soft voice of Zack rang around his head. "Watch your back". The words had not registered with him at the time as he'd been trying to weigh up the situation and show no fear of the threat. After the rush produced by the violence had died down he'd become anxious. The meet was supposed to have been routine, just a message for Carl. He would hand Zack a suitcase and take one in return. They had met like this several times. It was typical of the tasks he did for Carl. He would get a call once or twice a week and do a drop or back someone up for a beating, whatever was required. Sometimes he acted as chauffeur for the boss. Then at the end of the week he would get a roll of money, each time a little more than before.

Curtis had known of the infringement on Zack's turf but it was supposed to be secret, set up through another source to disguise their involvement. Somehow Zack had found out.

All the way back from the East End he'd been thinking it through. It did look like he had been set up for a beating by Carl, but he found this hard to believe. The man treated him like a kid brother. They could have words tonight.

"Where's my drink then?"

Curtis had forgotten his presence at the bar. He had been scanning the smoky corners of the room for Carl's features, making out fellow gang members and nodding acknowledgement, but not seeing the boss.

"Sure Ben, wanna beer yeah?"

"No, sah! Think I'll have a brandy to celebrate." He was smiling with pride. Curtis was slightly disgusted at the sight of his friend's smugness.

"It nothing big you know. I have to take care of myself like that every day sometimes. You like a schoolboy if you think that was a big deal."

Basically, this was a lie. Curtis had never used the chain before, except as a warning, and fights like that were rare with Carl's crew. Carl usually kept things civil. Curtis had been waiting for a chance to try the weapon though, and it had lived up to his hopes.

"Nothing to you maybe, but you a big gangster now, innit?"

There was a hurt tone to the lad's voice that reminded Curtis that it was his friend's action that had saved him. "Listen, I'm grateful for your help back there. Nothing was supposed to happen, I didn't think there'd be any hassle, right. Now, I have to talk with someone for a minute, so I meet you downstairs later."

Ben stared at him. He was tired of being talked to like a kid. Now even his friends were doing it, but he knew there was nothing to say but agree. Anyway, Mike would probably be downstairs on the floor and Ben wanted a chat with him.

"Sure. I see you down there. Beg that drink first though."

Maxine's was buzzing. He had to push his way down

through to the main room. The place was dark. There was no expensive light system, just a few simple spotlights and some alternating colours illuminated the dancers. They were mainly girls, moving low, enjoying the stares from the men crowded round the bar that ran down one wall of the club. It was still early, so the girls got in for nothing. The dance-floor ran the length of the room, squeezed between the bar and a wall that was topped by a thin balcony which you could get onto from the upstairs room. The balcony was unique to Maxine's as it had a waist-high parapet of steel topped by a row of thick glass squares reaching up to the ceiling. The insulation from the glass was so complete that you could stand looking over the crowded dance-floor and be in total silence, whereas beyond the glass the music boomed so loud it was hard to hold a shouted conversation. Huge, box-speakers were positioned all around the club floor, but up there in the balcony you could hear people chinking glasses and talking softly. The main room had been a small meeting hall a few years before, but Ben had been coming here at least once a month for over a year since it had been modernised. Recently he had been spending even more time here as he had a bit of money coming in from dealing. Curtis had advanced him a block of hash and Ben was selling it in small amounts, marking it up. He enjoyed having a few notes in his pocket and was thinking of selling on to another dealer. This was where Mike came in.

Mike was standing by the decks—but not *at* the decks. For the last hour he had been trying to ingratiate himself with the DJ, but the guy did not want to listen. All Mike wanted to do was have a spin on the system, but his wishes fell on deaf ears. He was looking exasperated when Ben caught sight of him, taking long pulls on a cigarette. His hair was a mess and his clothes hung from him like they were two sizes too big.

"Mike, you trying to get on the system again?" Ben had crept up on him and shouted the words like an angry schoolmaster. Despite the joke voice, his accent changed slightly speaking to a white guy, no matter who he was. Talking to Mike, he never had the easy roll of language he shared with Curtis.

"Christ, what you do that for? Frightened the life out of me nearly. How you doing anyway?" He spoke with slight difficulty and Ben could smell beer on his breath. Being drunk never affected the friendly and warm tone to his voice though. The two were old mates. Mike was the only true white friend he had.

"You wouldn't believe it Mike. I've been out East in all sorts of trouble. Kicked the fuck out of some guys there."

"Easy. What you doing out there? You know it's the land that time forgot, don't you? Wouldn't get me out there for a lot of money, I can tell you."

It was hard to talk over the noise of the thick beat pouring from the speakers so they were both shouting. Ben was happy to be with someone a bit more responsive than Curtis.

"Just a bit of a deal going off—which is something I wanted to talk about by the way. I may be in a position to help you make some money, man."

"Well we can talk it over at the bar, I think. This

bastard isn't gonna let me touch his gear, thinks I'm some tosser white guy who doesn't know the music."

Ben didn't want to state the obvious to his friend, tell him he could hardly expect to get on the system if he was white. He had no wish to knock Mike's hopes.

They moved to the far end of the bar, Mike carrying his record bag with some awkwardness through the crowd. He was careful not to let it swing into someone, but his clumsy step betrayed him once or twice and he had to mutter apologies. They found a clear spot in the corner at the end of the bar and the music wasn't so loud here, so they could talk.

"Who's buying then?"

Ben glanced at him with a smile. They had become friends years before at school. Mike was the tallest boy in the year but his frame was so light he had been a source of amusement for the crueller kids. He became a comedian to cope with the baiting and that still showed, even though he had been out of school for a while. He always had a broad grin on his face and was the first to laugh at a joke. However, he was far from stupid. The taunts at school had given him great strength of character and this combined with his intelligence made him an interesting companion. His one love was music. He collected albums obsessively and Ben had been round to his house many times to help him with the various tables and charts he compiled about the music. Reggae, lovers, ragga—these were his likes. You could find him in the local specialist shop where he worked, thumbing through the boxes like a huge stick insect, completely involved in the search for a certain track or artist. This was Ben's angle, as the addiction to records that Mike suffered from drained every penny he made. He only worked Saturdays and part-time and was always borrowing money, usually from Curtis.

Curtis treated Mike like a wounded animal. He felt he needed support. He had no intention of recovering the loans he made him. He just felt sorry for the guy, like he was the village idiot of West Park. Since teaming up with Carl though, Curtis had avoided Mike as he found it embarrassing to be linked with the gangling white guy. Not good for face. Mike was a bit hurt by it all, Ben suspected.

"So you've been out gangstering all night have you? You wanna be careful about all that you know. Curtis is hanging out with some types now. Could get a bit heavy soon for him I reckon."

"What you mean could get heavy? It already has. An' what do you mean some types? Honestly, you a bit slow, aren't you? He's deep in it by now. You should have seen him move tonight, man!"

"Yeah I can imagine."

"Man pull a chain and deal with the man, he . . ."

Mike looked away as though suddenly not interested. He was following the movements of a girl as she wound across the dance-floor. She was wearing the obligatory skin-tight outfit, but was one of the few girls who had the figure for it. Her legs were long and perfectly shaped. They swept up to a firm torso and flat stomach. She danced low. Mock but wise simulation of a sexual act. Mike was drooling. She brought her arms up across her stomach and over her breasts, all in time to the deep bass pulse and gravel-voiced rap of the track the DJ was spinning.

"Conversation stopper, huh?" Ben was taking in the sight himself. "More than that. She's dangerous, man."

"I know her, you know?" Mike sounded smug. He gulped at his beer and Ben thought he was trying to gain some prestige from this knowledge. He couldn't resist asking.

"How you know the sister then? I suppose she comes in your shop every now and again, does she? Like everyone else you have little chats with."

It was true that Mike was quite a socialite over the counter of the record store where he worked. A lot of youth would come in and he was a good source of information if they had a question about an artist or a release. Ben had seen it many a time. After a few minutes of chat, the victim would start laughing at Mike's inane jokes and then feel comfortable telling him where they lived and what they did with their time. He was a master at extracting information. He never went out on dates though. As well as being rather gangly and full of nervous laughter his face was an odd mix. The features didn't sit right. Girls liked his joking and good times, it just never got romantic as far as Ben could tell.

"Yeah, she's alright. Don't think she's seeing anyone at the moment either. Seems a waste really." His delivery wasn't coarse, but in the manner of a concerned, elderly relative. He was still watching her over the top of his glass.

"Well, get in there Mike. Or, if you don't think much of your chances then give me an introduction."

"Maybe later if your proposition's any good. I think money was mentioned."

"Yeah, I almost forgot. I was wondering if you'd like to come in with me on something. A bit of stuff I've got to sell."

"You must be joking. You mean that shit you've been peddling. Wouldn't touch it Ben."

"Come on, Mike. You can make money selling eighths."

"Naa, it's not for me that scene. I don't mind the odd puff, but not selling. Everyone's trying to deal at the moment—and it's illegal you know."

Ben laughed at the deliberate stupidity of the last remark. "So's nicking cars, but you do that . . ."

"Only when I'm pissed and can't afford a taxi. I haven't done that for years, anyway."

Curtis looked down at the two clowning friends. He was on the balcony above them checking the crowd for Carl. The face he wanted was nowhere to be seen in the undulating mass of people. They swayed and floated as though in silent trance to a beat he couldn't hear behind the glass. The thick scent of hashish wound up to him from a spliff between his fingers and he took another pull allowing the image beyond the glass to glow even more to his eyes. He had already checked with some of the others and there was an air of expectancy about them. Something was to be announced this evening when Carl got here, but nobody knew when he would arrive. He might already be in his rooms behind the bar, but the team were only allowed there by invitation, usually when he handed out the pay. In a stuffy little store-room full of boxes and crates Carl had his office. This was a table and two chairs. Behind him was a door through to a larger room, but Curtis had only seen glimpses of the interior when Carl came through the opening. He suspected it was a place for the boss to bed down when the journey home didn't appeal. Curtis had no idea where he lived. Carl was only seen at the club or in his car.

For a long moment Curtis considered going to speak with his friends, but felt it would be frowned upon, particularly tonight when he still had to quiz Carl about the events over the river. Anyway, Mike would want to borrow some money and he was a bit short at the moment. He seemed to be blowing large amounts on Amanda, his new girlfriend. Well, to call her his girlfriend was maybe an overstatement. He'd been chasing her for months and she was reluctant to confirm her feelings for him. They had met in the street, outside Bliss. She'd just wanted a light for her cigarette before getting in a car with two other girls, but he had taken her by the hand and led her back into the bar. His arrogance had interested her, and before she dragged herself away she gave him her number. Their meetings after that had been chaste, with her trying to extract information about his more violent encounters.

He suspected she got a perverse thrill from his lawless nature and means of earning money as she was from a conservative background herself. The money hand-outs from Carl had almost secured Curtis his first white girlfriend. She was powerfully attractive and too intelligent for him to charm into bed with his usual lines. He hadn't admitted to his friends that they had yet to sleep together. Her coyness had so far kept him interested. Curtis was surprised at himself. After tonight's business he would drop round on her and perhaps persuade her that the time was right. Musing on the tactic of a detached mood he realized she would see through it instantly. As he reflected on the likelihood of sexual union there was a soft tap on his shoulder and he spun round, muscles tensed.

"Easy, Curtis."

It was Carl.

He was so close Curtis could smell the brandy on his breath. Standing no taller than five feet, Carl still looked an imposing figure as he was barrel chested and thickset. Almost a cartoon character body was topped by a weathered face, hidden by the wide shades that he wore all the time. Curtis would have gambled he took showers in them. In any other person this might signify some insecurity but not with Carl. He wore them to keep you guessing. He was dressed in the usual leather jacket and suit trousers which were pressed impeccably as always. His domed head was completely bare which made it hard to guess his age, but Curtis was sure he was in his fifties. Not that this made him weak. Curtis had seen him deal with offenders—brute strength was his reputation. Carl had once told him he was carved from a hard wood. His cranium looked like black teak.

"What you saying, then? You back in one piece anyway."

So he was open about the danger of the encounter.

"Yeah, but it was a surprise. Me thought it was just a message. Then Zack set people on me."

"Well, you know. I have to be sure you can deal with the surprises too. Now I know you have fire in your blood. Zack a ras fool to mess with you." His voice was a bass growl, slow and thick. You could tell each word was thought through before he uttered it. He smiled wide and stepped back to the doors of the room behind. There was no chance to question him further. "Everyone here anyhow. I have something to tell you."

Curtis followed him through, staring at Carl's slumped back stretching the leather. It always amazed him. The man looked as though he could lift a horse. Through the glass doors the whole circle was waiting, about eight of them. The gang was unstructured apart from the fact that everyone knew Carl was on top. It always seemed the same with black gangs. The members were too independent to follow orders like an army unit. Part of the code was freedom from authority. A white gang would jump off a cliff if the boss said so, but not with this group. No man told you how to live, so the structure was loose. It was just the force of Carl's personality that kept them together. Curtis was the newest member and some of them had yet to accept him.

Most of them were in their late thirties. They were mellower than Curtis and happier to take the payroll. Well dressed to a man, in smart casuals or suits they sat around the room smoking and chatting in mur-

murs. As Carl strode in they slowly showed notice and broke off from conversation. Curtis felt like a lieutenant, backing up Carl's entrance to the staff room. He didn't fail to notice some of the glances and wondered if he had looked too high up for the leak to Zack, but none of these men knew he had been going over East tonight.

"Alright. Sit down and listen up."

Carl was only speaking normally but the volume of his voice was enough to drown out the remaining talk. He stood in the centre of the room, stepping over to the table every now and again to pick up his glass and take a sip.

"Me through with the things we working, got to try something fresh. There an outfit out of town approach me and we gonna try something with them. Up to now we been small dealin'."

One of the group sat back and sighed.

"We don't want no gun play, Carl, if that what you mean. We getting by alright as we is."

Obviously the gang out of town was known.

"Only getting by though. And soon others gonna step in our game. If it take gun play then that is the deal we dealin' in. You can step out now, if that too much for your belly."

"No sah. Me can play rough, if it tek so."

This was Ash. Curtis had always found him the most distant of the group. A tall, wiry man with a quick temper.

"Don't forget I have seen that side of things, man. It not an easy path."

"Well, that is what a go on, anyway. We doing a visit

next week. I pick the men later and we sort the details, but I had to tell you things might get a bit hard now. So, any man want an easy life better take retirement."

There was laughter at the phrase, but the group was tense. The work with Carl had been a soft ride so far. Some of them were thinking about the way youth was behaving these days and how things would change working with another group.

Carl had finished and he moved to leave. Curtis sensed that now was not the time to speak and did not follow as they all slowly wandered to the other room and the bar. Only he and Ash remained. From a low armchair Ash stared at him with his hands spread across the bottom of his face, covering his chin and mouth.

"Well, Curtis. Now you really gonna see the action. You want to play with the gangster, then? Young man like you should be looking high."

Curtis kept his eyes set on the man, keeping his body taught. Ash was trying to tempt him out to speak and his tone was sarcastic, accusatory. Better to leave him uncertain of his feelings. This was what Curtis had wanted all along. Now there would be change and progress. He wanted Carl up with the other gangs and the gun was the quickest way to earn respect.

"You keep quiet then. Remember though, me no pickney. I seen what gun do up front. I been behind the trigger boy."

Downstairs, the club was reaching capacity as it drifted towards morning. Ben was feeling charged now. All around him people seethed, moving to the beat, the girls bending low to the rhythm. The air was thick with smoke, lit up by the spinning lights and shining glass of the bar. Ben and Mike had been smoking spliff as they talked and the drug's subtle touch now wrapped around them as they swayed lightly to the music. Mike was flushed and bright-eyed, checking the crowd and the music. He turned to Ben and shouted. "You coming to the party tomorrow then?"

"Who's party? I didn't hear about any party."

Their conversation was staggered and Ben was surprised to hear his own voice. He hadn't guessed that he was so stoned, having been staring out at the crowd for some minutes.

"Round at Samantha's tomorrow night. It'll be a good one. We can go round together if you want."

Ben knew Samantha and was thinking about an embarrassing moment he had had with her in a hallway. Making a pass whilst drunk was one of his party tricks and she had been quite firm with her refusal. A slap in the face if he remembered correctly. "Don't know about that. I check you tomorrow in the afternoon."

"Oh don't worry about your little disagreement," said Mike. He was smiling a toothy grin and Ben was alarmed. "I think she quite likes you really. She told me to ask you anyway."

"How you know about that? Fuck, it's walls have ears round here, innit? That was private man."

"Ah, everybody knows."

Ben said nothing and turned away to show his anger. As he looked out on the crowd he could see the girl from earlier on that evening. She was dancing alone, moving in a slow, mesmeric pulse. Crouching low with her legs spread wide she dipped and rose, arms clasped above her head, face turned to the roof. Ben could see the lycra straining on her thighs as she mimicked riding a man. The image was so powerful he could think of nothing but the real thing and Mike's words about an introduction. He was about to turn back to his friend and bring the subject up when he saw a youth dressed in a silk shirt and cottons move up behind her and pass his arms around her waist. He pushed up close to her and broke into the rhythm of her dance but she was unresponsive. She broke her step and pushed him off. Her eyes were wide with fury and he could see her shout abuse at the would-be dance partner. With no warning he raised an arm and sent his palm flashing across her cheek, stunning the girl so she rocked back and almost fell.

Ben reared up and pushed his legs into motion. In a few seconds he was right next to them in a small clearing that had opened on the dance-floor. The excitement and victory of earlier that night, the hash and alcohol flooding his brain and the interest in the girl threw him into action. He pushed the youth to one side and stood between him and the girl. The man snarled at him. He was tough looking—short hair with a pattern of lines cut into it on the side, mean eyes and the tendons standing out on his neck. Ben wasn't sure what he was doing. He was making a stand again, as he had defending Curtis, trying to show the girl he was looking out for her, but his senses were dulled by the night's intake.

"Who you fuckin with?"

Ben stared at him with glazed eyes, swaying slightly. He expected the man to lunge at him, make a swing which he could counter and then he could floor him with a blow to the nose, marching out with the girl on his arm, indebted to him. However, as she whimpered behind him, Ben watched the youth drop his arm to his side and lift the edge of his shirt. It hung loose, a few inches below his waist and as he lifted it slowly, Ben saw a greasy metal plate, worn with fingering.

It was a gun handle.

Ben had never seen a gun up close. Just showing the weapon to him was enough. It established who was in power and he thought desperately how he could retreat. He had been in clubs when shootings had gone down, seen the awe of the crowd and the panic. That was always someone else getting blasted though. This was staring him in the face.

"You see, I tell you not to mess."

The man was gloating at the fear in Ben's eyes. His fingers curled around the butt of the revolver, relishing the rush of terror it had provoked.

"For man to play big out of him yard, always a mistake." It was Curtis, stepping out from the crowd, drawn up to his full height. Coming down to the main room he had seen the gap form in the dancers and guessed that a fight might be looming. Only curious, he had paced over and seen Ben protecting some girl and the bulge of a gun at the man's waist. Here he could pay back Ben's favour and build his reputation with Carl. A gun was big league and Carl had wanted to be sure his men could take it. Now he could show him that nothing turned him coward.

"Back off now, this between me an him. None of your concern, my friend." The man had noticed the steel in Curtis's face. He didn't want to draw the gun as once it was out it was likely he would have to use it and it was more a symbol to him than a real force. The sight of it alone had always gained respect in the past, but this new entrant on the game showed no concern. He stood solid, but relaxed, as though this was no big event. The coolness disturbed him but he hesitated in bringing out the revolver whilst Curtis broke his stance and stepped forward, face impassive. The man still paused, on the brink of acting, but he was too late.

Curtis changed from lazy movement to a sudden lunge, wrapping one arm round the man's chest and spinning him, reaching for the gun with his other hand. He easily overpowered the other, squeezing the air from his lungs with his metal grip and grabbing the handle. He let go and the man threw himself round to face him, back hunched and ready to fight now after the initial shock of the challenge, but Curtis slipped his fingers to the back of the man's head and pulled it down to the floor, lifting the exposed gun barrel with his other hand and ramming it into his mouth.

Even above the pounding music which had formed the backdrop to the fight, Ben heard the crack of metal on white enamel and the victim's muted sob. He sank to the ground, trying to breathe over the steel barrel and blood which together filled his mouth. Curtis had blazing eyes, as though the gun charged him with energy, power streaming up his arm. Ben had stepped back and held the girl protectively as the two battled, but watching Curtis now, he saw how his friend was gripped by some strange new lust. A glare contorted his face and the muscles in his wrist tensed as he tightened his finger around the trigger. "Curtis, settle down!"

The words did not register with him. He stared intently into the upturned eyes of the crouching man. He was superior, passing judgement on the offender.

"Settle down now!" Ben was by his side, hand on his shoulder. He shouted only inches from his ear and Curtis felt the outside world break through to him. His body slumped and he let go of the man's head, letting him stoop forward and tend to his broken face. "Curtis man. You get seize by a demon there. Come, let's go upstairs, yeah? I get you a drink."

He was still unresponsive, in a daze. He felt different now. The moment would stay with him for some time. "I'm alright Ben. Just helping you out. Man had it coming, bringing it down to the club, anyway."

They were pushing through the crowd which had returned to dancing after the incident. He wanted fresh air and some space and moved to the doors. Only as they were at the hallway did Curtis remember the gun, locked in his hand. "I have to get round to see a girl, Ben. I can drop you if you want."

He stared at the long barrel and bullet chamber of the revolver as he spoke. It felt like part of his arm.

"Yeah, I come back with you. I think you need to rest up a bit there, man."

Ben was helping Curtis to the car, arm round his

shoulders, thinking through the events of the night. He remembered the girl and reflected on the chances of meeting her some time in the future, thought about the first glimpse he had of her.

"Fuck! I almost got myself killed over the pussy there."

Curtis broke into laughter.

Four

The car was sweeping down the highstreet. The soft whine of the engine soothed him, carrying him to Amanda and comfort. She would be back from town by now. It was past midnight and he needed some attention after the strain of the day. If only he had accepted the invitation to come with her then he could have avoided the fight with Zack and the incident at the club, but Carl had called at the last moment with the task and he had been duty bound to go. The ache of exhaustion ran up and down his body and he was still confused by the emotions the gun had brought out in him. It lay in the boot where he had thrown it, covered by a blanket.

Ben had been ranting on, all the way back to his house and Curtis was glad to have him out of the car. A lecture was not what he needed. He pushed down on the accelerator, thinking of the girl waiting for him and his chances of sharing her bed.

Ben crept up the drive to his house, attempting to be silent but failing due to his swimming head and wobbly legs. As he pulled out a key for the front door he lost his balance and stumbled against it, ringing the bell with his shoulder. A light came on inside and he groaned, anticipating the arrival of his tired father. He stretched up and cleared his throat as the door opened, revealing a man in his forties wearing a dressing gown.

"So you come in at last then. Well, I been waiting to talk with you."

He wasn't angry. Ben had never seen his father angry, only frustrated or depressed when his actions had upset him. He would adopt a sad tone as a means of punishment and it was very effective, but tonight Ben had been through too much for a sermon.

His father looked weary, with tired eyes and slumped shoulders. He had all the life beaten out of him.

"Oh not now, Dad. We can talk over breakfast." Ben was pulling off his jacket and making for the stairs to his room.

"Breakfast! When you at breakfast? You never up

before lunch and I have to work you know. Down the bloody school every day."

His father was a technician at the local comprehensive. Ben had spent years trying to avoid him round the classrooms and passages and the situation had put enormous strain on their relationship. He had never really forgiven him for working at the same school he attended.

"I know you have to work every day, I know you feed and clothe me, I know all that."

"Well you can listen to me then if you know so much. It three in the morning Ben, three you hear? Where you been all night? We got to talk about you staying here because I don't think it doing you any good. Six months now since you stop school, and no job, no training. What you goin' to do boy.?"

"I told you, I been looking around I'll find something soon."

"Well make soon, sooner, you know." The tone had been the same for as long as Ben could remember. His father had always struck him as a sad figure who worried about the smallest things in life. Sometimes he could turn his negative view of life into a cutting black humour, but he was in preacher mode right now.

Ben had no answer for his questions. He was waiting to see what came up in terms of a job opening or studies for some skills, but nothing had appealed to him yet. Why couldn't he enjoy himself at the same time? His father was walking away to the kitchen, probably for some of the warm milk that he claimed he had to drink to sleep at nights, giving Ben the chance to slip away.

However, this time Ben followed him down the hallway, not prepared to let him paint his son a loss once more. "It not easy you know. Most of my friends are out running with gangs or making money themselves with things you wouldn't believe . . ."

"You'd be surprised what I'd believe, son." He had turned in the narrow kitchen and reached to his nightgown. He pulled a small plastic bag from his pocket. It was Ben's stash. "What this then? Symbol of your entrepreneurial spirit, is it?"

His face was dark, but not completely without humour. The expression confused Ben. Was he getting some kick pointing out his son's failings or was it that he himself used to enjoy a smoke when he was a youth? His father was a mystery to him.

"So you wanna smoke some, then? Wanna sit down with me now and get high?"

Ben was speechless for a moment. This was a cruel tactic.

"We can talk tomorrow, Dad. I'm too tired to deal this. Give it back to me, now."

His father handed the package over with a shrug and Ben made for the stairs.

"You only gonna get in worse trouble with that you know Ben."

He made no answer, but strode into his room and pulled the door shut. Downstairs his father pulled up a chair by the kitchen table and fell into it. He blew out a long gush of air and thought about sleep's sweet kiss removing his worry.

*

The lights were still on at Amanda's flat. She lived in the top rooms of a large house and he had to walk several flights of stairs to reach her door. As he knocked he could hear soft music and he was relieved that she was not in bed already. With any other girl he would have had no qualms about turning up in the early morning, but Amanda was not the type to tolerate such actions. Curtis knew he was skating on ice with this girl. He had to watch his step.

"Oh Curtis, you're here at last." She stood in the doorway, still dressed for town. He was relieved at the warmth in her voice. "Come in. Bob and Sarah are here having a drink."

He followed her, resisting the temptation of taking hold of her dress and pulling her back to him. He didn't want to chat with her friends, but was playing polite so he had no choice. As he turned the door the couple on the sofa rose to meet him. They were typical of Amanda's friends, well dressed, a little ugly, but healthy looking. Bob had the neat haircut and weak handshake, probably worked for a bank, and Sarah looked the theatrical type. She had long tangled hair and a flowery dress draped over a small, plump torso. He decided they'd been waiting for his arrival like visitors to the zoo.

"So this is your toyboy then, Manda." Sarah had a thin, nasal voice that lifted up at the end of the sentence.

Amanda flushed, then put her arm around his shoulders, obviously proud of her new asset. He felt young in their company though they were only a few years older.

"That is not how I would have termed myself, Sarah." When he wanted to he could adopt a pure, Queen's English accent and the soft tones caused a little stir in the trio.

"So how would you term it then, Curtis?"

He felt apart from them. His dress and colour confused them and he hated the inquisitive gaze, as though he wasn't human.

"I think it's hard to define our relationship."

They abandoned the questioning as they realised he was quite able to counter their remarks. Amanda filled him a glass of wine and sat next to him in an armchair opposite the others. After a few moments of silence they began talking of the film they had seen that evening and how good the restaurant was afterwards. Curtis stared at the wall as Bob theorized on the symbolism of the movie, thinking how he found abstract conversation circular and dull. He wondered if Bob had ever hit anyone or felt a gun in his hand. It was only down in the car. He thought about bringing it up to show them. Amanda would love it. Her interest in his dark side was the link they had. Bob and Sarah had none of her craziness.

He relaxed as he drank more wine and began joining in with the conversation matching their intellect easily. After twenty minutes they said farewell, Bob giving Amanda a kiss that Curtis found rather too lingering. He nodded goodbye without standing up.

"You could have made more of an effort."

She was standing in front of him, slightly angry. The fabric of the dress hid nothing of her curves. Her breasts stuck out prominently as she stood hands on hips and he let his eyes roam. Her face was strong, set with a light complexion and scarlet lips. Long brown hair stretched past her shoulders.

"Well, if you put me on show like some animal what do you expect?"

Now she moved off and started cleaning up the glasses and mess from the visit. She muttered questions about his day and such, but he was not listening. He studied her legs and bottom, thinking only of when she would allow him to peel away her clothes and sink into her.

Noticing his gaze she wandered back and sat down on his lap. She was clever enough to know that eventually he would tire of waiting for her, but she still felt unsure about Curtis. When it happened she wanted him to be around for a while and not just scratch her off as another conquest and this was why she had held out on him so far. He would have been interested in her dreams about him, she knew that.

"So, am I your guest tonight then?"

"Well I have to be at work early." She saw how frustrated he was by her remark. "Soon darling, don't worry."

"Soon not tonight though, is it?"

She let it drop for a few seconds and then kissed him on the cheek. "Curtis."

"Hmm!" She was draped around him now and he lifted his hand further round her legs towards her thigh.

"Do you think we're going to last, Curtis?"

"What kind of a question is that, you're still not ready to sleep with me are you? How can I know how

I feel when you don't trust me enough to sleep with me?"

"It's not just sleeping with me, is it? I mean, is that what this means to you?"

She would always start with the meaning of it, and the fact they had done nothing yet frustrated him. She wanted to talk and never do anything but he couldn't bring himself to push her into it.

"Look, any other girl, I would have left if she'd held out on me like you. Of course you mean something to me, but I can't make predictions, Amanda. We have to see how it goes, you know."

She was amused at his speech. Maybe it would work out with him if she could have both sides of him, the hard man and the hidden thinker.

"I just need a little more time, then I'll be sure."

He stood up, lifting her with him. He wanted to carry her to the bed in her room, but let her down gently to the carpet, knowing she would only shout at him if he took her in that direction. How much time was he going to devote to this and was he really getting involved in something other than wanting her body? There had been too much confusion already for the day.

"Look, I'm going back to my flat. I don't want to stay up all night with you teasing me on the sofa. We're not kids, Amanda. I'll call you."

He walked out to the hallway and heard the door close behind him, but not before she whispered, "Talk to you soon, Curtis."

Five

Ben paced round the kitchen barefoot, making himself a cup of tea. It was a dreary morning outside. Through the windows that ran along one side of the room he could see an overcast sky set against the rooftops of the next street. He cursed—the clock showed that it was past eleven and he had hoped to catch his father to have a talk with him. He must have left hours before and Ben was not sure whether he would be in around dinner time. A few seconds' thought made it clear that there was no way he was going into the school to talk with him. That was the last thing he needed. He did have to ask him about the conversation the night before, though. Ben had been charged to say the least. He had also drunk a fair amount of beer with Mike.

The thought of Mike caused him to mutter another expletive. Ben remembered that he'd run out without saying whether he was going to the party or not. People were always forgetting about Mike. Anyway, he could make amends for that later, but now he was thinking of his father's words. He had definitely mentioned something about Ben's future stay in the house and this was scary. It was one thing being independent and having your own life, but Ben was not on the point of wanting to move out, far from it. He was making enough from selling a lump of hash every so often to run around and have a drink, but he had no savings or real income. Some friends of his had asked him to come in on thieving stereos and phones from cars, but Ben knew he was not cut out for that sort of thing, even though the money was good. Curtis had his own place, but he had put a lot of time and money into it. It had been a dive when he'd first got it. Curtis had the patience and a bit of cash, so he could make a go of it, but the thought of being cooped up in a little bed-sit didn't appeal to Ben—and that was what he would end up with, he was sure.

He had always thought there would be a place for him here. His mother had died when he was an infant and despite their differences, Ben thought of his father and himself as a team. Now that was at risk and the only way to keep Pops happy was to get a job. It was a terrible prospect.

Ben was skilled at being lazy. He brooded over his tea about a method of persuading his father that he was a right-thinking member of society. This was going to be difficult when the evening before his dad had casually produced a quarter-weight of finest Afghanistan black, found on his son's floor. Ben still owed Curtis the money for it and was slowly smoking more than he was selling, but this didn't worry him. Curtis was easy about such things. His father was not too concerned about the hash. He was oddly liberal about some aspects of life and Ben suspected he'd been fond of a puff himself in his youth. His concern would be his belief that after the hash comes a harder drug and then harder still. Ben was well aware that the harder the drug the greater the profit for the seller, but he had no intention of moving up from hash. That was the gangster scene and he would leave that well alone. He just wanted to chill with a good hit, make a few pennies and think things over for a while. He would try to explain this to his father when he next saw him.

Having made up his mind that all was well now, despite having reached no solution, he hurried up to his room for his grooming. Once Ben had thought about something for a few minutes he considered the problem solved. He wasn't good at coming to grips with reality. Most of the time it was pretty dull anyway, he found.

He admired himself in a full length mirror—baggy, patched jeans with bursts of pastel colours, a black T-shirt, still with a tight neck and a logo jacket that cost serious money. He positioned a plain baseball cap on his head and smiled to himself. *You look criss and you smell sweet boy*!

Stuffing some change in his pocket he ran down the stairs and along the hall to the front door.

He was heading for the leisure centre, though he had no desire to exercise whatsoever. This was a throwback to his schooldays when he was down here every lunch-time and afternoon after lessons. The centre had been his introduction to fighting and romance, on the schooldays level anyhow, but he still came down periodically and always bumped into a few friends just hanging out. It had been his arena and he remembered some of the victories and losses of those days. Ben missed them more than he admitted. Many of his peers had floated off into jobs or to college and the longer he left it, the more it seemed an impossible task to deal with the trials of real life. He was not going to dwell on it though today.

He crossed the main road, weaving through the crawling traffic and ran eagerly over to the glass entrance hall. Doors triggered by overhead sensors slid open for him and he strolled across to the restaurant. He liked the atmosphere, glass and chrome every-where. The reception area was spacious, with a domed roof and white tiled walls. There were benches scat-tered round the edges, each with a large plant at either end, giving the whole space the look of a sophisticated greenhouse. After buying a soft drink he went out to the reception hall again and checked faces for some-one he knew. The place was busy. People used it as a short-cut through to the shopping precinct as there were doors at the back that ran straight through to it. There was a continual stream of people. He saw no-one he knew at first then recognized a pair of seated girls. He wandered over, smiling. They were from the year below him at school, probably on their lunch break.

"Hello there, girls. Me thought you look lonely so I come an' join you."

"I remember you. You were that friend of Curtis, innit?"

This was the feisty one, nose turned up in a flirtatious sneer. The other girl was shy, laughing behind a cupped hand and Ben found her more attractive. He reckoned she was a virgin for sure. He wasn't too happy about Curtis getting a mention like that, but he had somehow attained almost cult status with a group of girls at the school. They found his mature reserve irresistible, even though he had left almost two years before. The legend lived on due in part to the fact that he cruised the area in his car. He was still a face they remembered. Ben decided to play them at their own game.

"Who this Curtis then? Me never hear a no Curtis."

"Oh yeah? Well, I don't believe you. You is Ben and you his friend if I remember."

"Me think you have amnesia den."

They were all laughing and Ben thought he may as well push his luck. He was still standing in front of them, swaggering a bit, knowing he looked good. He aimed his questions at the shy girl who was too nervous to look at him straight on.

"So, you know Samantha then?"

"I know a Samantha, but I don't know if it the one you know, do I?"

"She having a party tonight then, this Samantha you know?"

"Maybe she is, what's it to you then?"

"Well, I want to know if I'm gonna see you there, don't I?"

"What, you asking me? Big man like you." The sarcasm took him unawares.

"Girl have a tongue on her. So, what you saying then?"

"Maybe, but I have to go now, if you see me, then you see me." They jumped up and walked off giggling.

Ben asked himself if he was too old to be flirting with schoolgirls and decided he probably never would be.

Mike was loitering in the storeroom as always, searching for some long deleted record. The shop was tiny, just one small room and a service desk, but the rows of shelves in the back room stretched back for thirty yards or more and Mike knew every inch of them. They held thousands of records and what they didn't have could be ordered in a day, so the shop was well known by determined record buyers.

"Service my good man, service!"

Mike was working alone today and hadn't been watching the shop door so he missed Ben creeping in. The bellowing startled him but as soon as he saw who it was he smiled and marched back to the counter from the vinyl graveyard.

"You pisstaker. Had me worried for a second. And what the fuck happened last night, by the way? You getting all heroic with that girl and Curtis stepping in, walking out on me, I don't know. I should blank you for that." He was still fingering a record sleeve, examining it as he spoke, turning it with adoration.

"You and records, it too much you know. What time we going down the party then?"

"Not till late, yeah? Oh, so you changed your mind then?"

"Well, me meet a real sweet thing just a while ago and I asked her along. Can't go standing her up now, can I?"

"Wouldn't be the first time. Anyway, what about Samantha? She ain't gonna be too happy."

"She had her chance and she blew it."

Mike burst out laughing. "Go, Casanova."

"Well, who you taking then?" He wished he hadn't said it immediately.

A wave of sadness flashed across Mike's face and then he recovered, as he always did. "Got no plans to take a girl. Happy just getting drunk again, I think."

They talked about the gun from the night before. Ben only remembered the broad events and Mike filled him in on the details. He was flattered by the image of himself, the protector.

"I spoke to her after you pissed off. She was looking for you to give you a big kiss thankyou."

"Fuck off!"

"No really, she was grateful. The guy really freaked

her out when he came over. She's not as street as she looks, I tell you."

They had shared a few words at the club, it was true, but nothing much had been said. This was Mike trying to be important in the conversation. The girl had probably forgotten him already.

"Work out some way for me to meet with her then, Mikey boy. I have to run see someone. Meet you in Bliss about ten, how does that sound?"

Bliss was their usual drinking choice before a club if they were going out. It was a cross between a pub and a wine-bar in style, smart but not stuck-up and it tolerated drinkers at the fringes of eighteen. Ben liked the music there as it was a bit more jazz tip than the hard ragga he listened to most of the time.

"Sound good, Ben. Take it easy."

Ben was running around today. After leaving Mike he had to jump a bus which crossed over to Sheltham and then walk a bit. It was rougher here than his yard. Most of the houses were run down or vacant and the estates he passed were blocks bunched together as though in conspiracy to force out the sunlight. Back in West Park there were still breaks of green and a few proud home-owners. He couldn't imagine the inhabitants of Sheltham worrying too much about litter or a stray dog crapping in the road. Even the shops looked tired out and abused. There was nothing for it in a place like this but to get out of your head now and again and that was why he was here. He had a quarter in his chest pocket and he was well aware of it. Coming over on the bus he began to feel a bit nervy. Best to get in and out fast, he thought to himself—he was already a fair walk from the bus stop. He stopped at a row of small terraces and checked the address.

The door was the worst shade of yellow he could imagine and even that was starting to peel. It was the standard broken-down porch of a decaying house and he had seen plenty. There was the frosted glass, chipped in the corner, weeds breaking through the concrete path up to the door and faded curtains clenched tight to protect the front room from prying eyes. He knocked firmly, but was feeling rather apprehensive as he knew some of the local boys and the things they got up to. The Sheltham youth had nothing to lose.

There was a shuffle in the corridor. Adam from Bliss had told him about the buyer a few days before, but he was known as being unreliable, it was just that Ben needed the money. Most of his friends wanted weed not this hash and he was having to pursue some desperate avenues to get rid of it. Adam knew some odd people.

The door opened a crack, still on the chain, and a girl's hand crept round the edge.

"Yeah, what do you want?"

It was a flat voice, devoid of character, as though numbed somehow. Ben guessed she was stoned already.

"I'm supposed to see Paul about something."

"Right, come in." She was more excited now. At the mention of the man's name she had perked up.

The door opened and he saw her retreat down a thin hallway full of junk. There were boxes of newspaper and cardboard, some tools and stereo equipment. He saw a bike tyre sticking out from under it all. Up in the ceiling there was a bare bulb, a low wattage sun for the corridor.

"Well, it's got something about it, I have to say."

He had followed her into the living room which was mysteriously located at the back of the house. The design of the building puzzled him. Initially impressed by the tonnes of trash in the hall he was bowled over by the main room which made the earlier sight appear trivial.

This room was packed with junk. The ceiling was touched by pile after pile of random garbage, bright pink fabric, silver foil in large lumps, broken bits of furniture and roadsigns. There was a window, but you could see no light, just the curtains at the top. That wall was covered with thousands of short cables, odd tools like welding apparatus and boxes full of shiny bits of metal. Across the ceiling of the room, surrounded by the walls of garbage and miscellaneous junk, there was a billowing fold of silky fabric. It puzzled him for a second, but then he saw it was a parachute, tacked up in the corners of the room and with a faint glow behind it. This was the only illumination and meant the space was covered in a twilight gloom. Seated amidst the kingdom of junk was Paul, settled back in a bubbling armchair, the stuffing trying to burst from every seam.

He was hairy. A mane of a beard and a fringe from hell. Ben wondered if he had ever visited a barber. He wore a jumper and faded jeans, which made it impossible to judge his physique. It was too dark to really take in his face, but Ben thought he was probably quite young. He was expecting him to speak and stood uneasily in the centre of the room where there was a small clearing showing the brown carpet's original design. It was just big enough for him and the girl to stand in.

He looked at her now. She was quite short but had a nice figure swathed in loose, pastel cottons. Her hair was fair, maybe even blonde in daylight and there was a hint of beauty about her. She had a crazy look in her eyes, but her other features were nun-like. Her mouth and nose were perfect, pretty and pink, and her jaw swept tightly down to a long neck. As he stared at her he noticed she was staring back with no look of surprise in her face.

"Most men find me attractive." Her voice had woken up now and taken on a soft lilt.

"Really. And how do you feel about that?"

"Oh I don't mind." She had a careless edge to her voice, almost childish. Now she turned back to Paul. "He's here Paul, the man with the black."

Paul stirred. He had been staring at them both without making a sound, but he propped himself up in the chair now and leant forward.

"Is it good then?" Paul sounded like a smart-ass public school boy or an RAF corporal, defying the ruin of his house and his clothes. "Is it the best I've ever smoked?" This was a sarcastic tone, mimicking the sales-talk of a bad pusher. "Because the quality is important to me, you understand?"

Ben had never been interrogated about hash before. He had only been selling it a month or two and most of his customers were happy to get their hands on anything that burnt.

"Well it gets me stoned. That's all I can say, you know. Smoke a bit if you want."

Paul didn't hesitate. He clicked his fingers and the girl stuck her hand out like a greedy puppy. Ben dropped a pea-sized ball of the hash into her outstretched palm and watched as she hurried over to her master. Paul had reached down into one of the many junk piles, rummaged around for a second and pulled out a long, glass tube with a bulbous end. His fingers packed the roll of dope into a silver slot and then pulled a lighter from his grime-covered jeans. Ben was watching every action, fascinated. After flicking the wheel a few times he got a light and started to burn the hash, sticking the open end of the tube up to his mouth. It disappeared into his beard. Ben heard a muted sucking sound and watched the smoke curling up the tube, through the bulge of the pipe, which from the slurping sounds that he heard he guessed was full of water or some liquid. It was a spectacle.

When the tube was packed tight with smoke, the man removed the end of the tube from his mouth and muttered to the girl. "Astrid, my sweet."

She bent down and kneeled next to him. Taking the pipe in both hands she took a mighty heave on it and tossed her head back. After a few seconds keeping it in her lungs, she blew out a massive cloud of thick, white smoke and Ben smelt the powerful scent of the drug floating in the air. He could only see the girl's back but could make out little tremors in her skin as though she were shaking. Then she rolled off her knees on to her side and sat there beaming at him across the brown carpet. He was still standing in the middle of the room, fidgeting.

"Wanna go on the headsucker, old boy?" Paul was leaning over, pushing the pipe to him, strands of smoke whisping from the end.

"No, you're alright thanks, I just sell the stuff."

"Suit yourself then."

Now he repeated the slow fill of the pipe and indulged himself. As he breathed deep on the smoke his whole chest expanded. Ben thought he would explode and wanted to shield his face. He held it in for what seemed a minute or two, until his lungs were bursting, then let out a rush of air, but with very little smoke, most of it having been absorbed into his lungs. He wiped his lips with the back of his hand and fell back into the armchair.

"Good stuff, old bean. Grade A."

Ben was getting impatient. He wanted to get out of this madhouse. The girl looked comatose and Paul was obviously from another planet.

"You can have the quarter for forty then if you like it, yeah."

He sounded the nervous business man, not sure of his client and therefore blushing slightly.

"Oh I don't know about buying it from you. I mean the stuff grows on fucking trees, you know."

"Come again? You mean you not taking it from me . . ." His temper was rising. "I come all the way to shithole Sheltham, you try the stuff, say you like it and then don't want to pay. Who the fuck d'you think I am, fucking dope Santa or something? You pay forty for the quarter, twenty-five for an eighth, which one do you want?"

"Well I don't want either actually, I'm quite happy as I am."

Ben walked the few paces up to the chair and lifted a fist to Paul's face. "Joke's over, asshole. Give me some money."

This was the only way he knew how to deal with the situation. He had to have a sale today to be able to go out tonight and Paul was it. Ben knew his threat was largely a front, but was gambling that Paul wouldn't be so sure.

"You can have Astrid I suppose. She must be worth something to you." Paul was still relaxed. The threat of violence had not broken through to his stoned thinking and he had uttered the words in a casual manner.

Ben turned to the girl on the floor out of sympathy for her being stuck with a guy like Paul but was stunned to see her beckoning him to her side. What was with these people?

"Are you serious? You'd fuck me right here on the floor? In front of him?" He was wide-eyed and looking a bit boyish from shock.

"Why not. He says it's OK and we do have a very free relationship." Her words were broken, hard to decipher. She was so out of it she was somewhere between complete pleasure and utter disorientation, probably not even sure where she was.

Ben had to get out. He would have wanted her in other circumstances, but not like this, with her deranged boyfriend watching. Even as he thought to himself how best to escape, she rolled over again and landed at his feet. Like a snake her hand pounced on his crotch and she pulled her mouth up level with it. Paul was smiling way back in the armchair.

"No, no, it's not my scene, lady. Get off me will you."

She was yanking at the buttons on his trousers, pulling deftly at the light underwear. Her body was slumped around his legs, he didn't want to hit her, but he couldn't move and she was working her way into his pants. As he thought about clipping her ear with the side of his palm she broke through to flesh and to his horror, pulled him into her mouth.

The shock of her bare-face intimacy and Paul's muted chuckles in the background were too much for him to know how to react. After only a few seconds he was almost fully erect inside her mouth, standing helplessly on the brown carpet surrounded by trash. Despite the madness of the situation he was teetering either way, not so anxious now to free himself. His hands began to slip round to the back of her head to guide her movements, but a last thought broke through his lust and he pushed her away. There was no way he was going to perform in front of the lunatic in the armchair throne.

"Oh, why d'you do that?" It was Paul, putting on a child's voice.

Ben tied his jeans and turned to him, bent forward, and from there sent a vicious uppercut into the man's beard. His head flew back with a jerk. Ben had exorcised his frustration at the whole incident with the punch. He didn't want to really savage him, the punch just let out some steam. Paul dropped his head to one side and panted into the arm of the chair. He turned to the girl. She was still sitting there, waiting for him to do whatever he wanted with her. He had the feel of her mouth as a memory, but that was how it would stay for now. With the dumb grin on her face she looked a lobotomy candidate.

He pushed past her roughly. "I might come and see you some time, you never know, when we can be alone maybe."

"I'd like that."

It occurred to him that she was maybe the most compliant woman he had ever met, what he imagined it was like back in caveman days. A couple like that were certifiable. He walked out into the hall and down to the door. As he stepped out onto the street he pushed a hand back through his hair with relief.

"Crazy fuckers."

The room was dark but he knew it was day outside. He lay on top of the bed, staring over at the bookshelf on the opposite wall. The third shelf up supported his phone. He was debating whether to call her at work or not. He decided to wait on her and reached out an arm to a small table by the bed, covered in smoking debris. There were small wraps of hash and weed, broken cigarettes and papers for rolling spread over a few magazines and the pieces of paper he did his accounts on. A circular ashtray held the stub of a joint he had been smoking the night before. He lit it and lay back on the bed, feeling the rush to his head. Curtis never got up before having a smoke. It kept him level, making his mood easy. He blew smoke-rings at the ceiling.

He had heard about the party and was thinking of going. It was around five already, he had slept right through the day after his exertions, but he had nothing to do in particular so he could just relax until the evening.

Curtis would not have been interested in the party if Amanda had invited him to sample her fleshy delights the night before, but it had been a while since he had been with a woman and this seemed like a good opportunity for it. He knew some of the girls there held him in awe. Maybe he could take one of them for a late night drive and suggest dropping by his flat. Here he had all the ingredients for seduction.

The hallway ran into a large living-room and this in turn had an arch through to the bed in which he was lying now. It was one walk through the flat to his lair. Many had fallen prey to this route in late night, drunken stumbling. Amanda had walked over to his sofa and sat down with her legs crossed. For the first time in his sexual career he was thinking about this one girl having some great importance. There was always the chance of her discovering some indiscretion of his, or even worse, how would it make him feel about her if he slept with someone else? He didn't want to damage that.

This was ridiculous. Curtis had been sleeping with girls for years now. He had just got the flat together after a year in a shabby dole-hotel room and he should be entertaining every night. The last month though he'd been running around after Amanda. Before, he had always had two or three options for a night's company, but those girls no longer appealed. He had gradually cut them off as he tried to phase Amanda into his life. She was an altogether more interesting subject than some giggling teenager.

He sat up in the bed and dropped the roach of the joint into the ashtray. Maybe a shower would clear his head. In his boxers and a white T-shirt he strode across the bedroom to the main room. The carpet felt deep and soft to his feet. Over by the front window, now shielded by a thick cream curtain, he fiddled with the stereo, stuck in a tape and turned the volume dial right up.

Bass flooded the flat with a low boom. Then the drums came in, crisp and quite thin with a shrill bell on every beat. Finally the voice crashed across the mix. It was a low, dirty chant, the man reaching back into his throat for the gravel sound. Curtis went into a crouch and started moving round the flat, miming to the tune. The music made him feel alive, the energy from the speakers charged him up on top of the puff he had just smoked. He made for the shower, still moving in time to the track, and flicked the light on in the bathroom. He would spend an hour or two preparing himself and see how he felt, but just before he stepped under the gush of water he made sure the door was slightly open so he could still hear the phone. He smiled to himself. *You got it bad Curtis*.

Bliss was just off the highstreet, down a narrow one-way side road, so you tended to get a crowd of locals and people who met here regularly rather than much passing trade. Ben was early and the bar wasn't yet full, so he slipped into a booth and started turning over the day's events in his mind.

He was having second thoughts about the Sheltham duo. Maybe he should have let the girl finish what she started—he had a dull ache in his groin now and decided it was due to not coming after being aroused by the girl. The image of beating the crap out of Paul was more appealing now as well.

Ben had no money. He had been relying on the sale of the quarter for some cash and the chances of selling it now were remote. He recognized at least two dealers from where he was sitting and they wouldn't be too happy if he was to start proffering his wares around the bar. So, he had to sit without a drink, waiting for Mike. The chances of a loan from him were sure to be nil, indeed, Mike would probably want something from Ben.

He studied the bar. It was a long L shape with the bar itself following the bend. The booths ran down one wall next to windows covered by blinds and there was a clutch of small tables spread around the room. Even though it was far from being full the air was thick with smoke and the conversation was loud. People had to talk up to be heard over the music, a seventies rare-groove thing he didn't recognize.

After what seemed a lifetime ducking the gaze of the bar staff, Mike gambled through the doors and squeezed his frame onto the seat opposite him. He was wearing the same stuff as he had on in the shop earlier that afternoon whilst Ben had sneaked in at home to throw on a fresh shirt.

"Boy, you scruffy you know?"

"Oh, fuck off will you? I've had a hard day. The boss came in and gave me shit about some missing order."

"Missing to your pocket then, is it?"

"If only, Ben. I'm bust, mate. Anyway, I bought you plenty of beers down Maxine's, get us a drink in!"

Ben was amused by his assumption. In making the demand, Mike had turned away, not quite able to deal with being assertive.

"What with then? I have no money myself. We a couple a paupers."

Mike looked sincerely pained. "What about your drop this afternoon? You must have something left from that."

"Me never sell it. I don't even want to talk about that." He wasn't sure if the experience would paint him badly as the anecdote was a bit sensitive. Mike would be alarmed by the blow-job element anyway, he was sure of that. Ben had to smile.

"So what we gonna do then? Have to take something to the party."

"I still have it on me."

"No, something to drink I mean."

"Hmm."

The two friends thought for a moment in silence. Mike rubbed his chin as he brooded. Ben could think of nothing but the twenty-four pence he had in his pocket.

"We have to roll someone."

The suggestion stunned him. "You what? You mean a mugging?"

"Well, there's plenty of pissheads wandering round at this time. Just have to scare them a bit and they hand over the wad."

Mike was straight-faced, but Ben expected him to burst out laughing any second. He couldn't be serious.

"Or if you'd rather go home to Daddy and a night in . . . We can't go to the party without drink."

He was right and Ben had a strong urge to see if the girl from the centre would turn up. He was surprised by Mike's hardness though. Seemed like everyone was getting a bit tough-edged these days.

"Well, how we do it then? I don't want to get myself messed up having fisticuffs with a wino."

"No, you hide and I just ask for a light or something. Then when they're off guard you jump out and the fucker'll be so scared he hands over his wallet and we run off into the night. Perfect plan wouldn't you say?"

"Brilliant, Mike, it can't go wrong."

"Never mind the piss-take, let's go have a look."

"You for real on this?"

"Yeah, man."

"Well if Mikey talking 'bout a mugging then things must be bad. Come now."

They walked down the highstreet, past the Kebab shops and take-aways and started checking the side-streets for lone walkers.

"Should we do this in our own area man? I mean, what if they know us?"

"Don't be stupid, Ben. There are millions of people in this city. We won't be that unlucky."

"Have you done this before then?"

"Course not." Mike sounded offended.

They were walking down a more residential street now and the lighting was very bad. Ben had some friends who had done a few muggings and they had told him a little about it, but it had always made him feel a bit disgusted. This was getting a bit serious for him. They had mentioned that corners were best as you could make an escape and you had more chances of coming across potential victims.

He suggested this to Mike, but once he had said it he knew he was not going to be able to go through with it. "Think I might have to duck out on you, Mike."

"What? You going soft, big gangster like you? We don't have to hurt anyone, do we? Just scare them a bit an' then we're set for the night."

Ben wasn't listening. He had noticed the shape of a man lumbering towards them about a hundred yards off. He looked drunk as his walking was staggered and unsure.

"How about him then?"

"You've changed your mind in a hurry haven't you? Look, get round the wall and come out when I stop him."

Mike sounded a bit too leader-like for Ben but he followed the instructions. They were in front of a row of houses with low front walls and Ben crouched behind one, just inside the gate as Mike prepared to face the oncomer. This was crazy, the guy could be anyone, could be a karate expert for all they knew. The random element was quite a buzz.

The drunk had reached Mike on the pavement. Ben

couldn't see either of them but was close enough to hear the man's laboured breathing.

"Got a light mate?"

There was no response but the sound of him fumbling in his overcoat. The tension rose up in Ben and he stood, stepping out onto the pavement. Mike had drawn the man along a few paces so Ben was facing a rounded back and hunched shoulders. He must have been in his fifties as his hair was very thin and going grey where it remained. Mike suddenly reared up and shoved the man in the chest, pushing him back on Ben. He tried to turn and run, which would have been laughable he was so inebriated, but catching sight of Ben behind him his face dropped in submission.

"Hope you've got some money for us or we're gonna turn your face inside out."

Being in control like this was giving Ben a rush, but the cold voice of Mike seemed so different from his usual tone it scared him a little. Ben was used to violence, threats, intimidation, but only within his own circle, not picking on some innocent. He should have backed out from the start.

"Yeah take it, I don't want any bother with you boys." He was trying to laugh, to relax them.

Ben studied Mike over the man's shoulder and was relieved to see calm and no dementia such as had gripped Curtis when he fondled the gun. At least this wasn't going to his head.

From inside his overcoat he produced a wallet and simply gave it over to Mike, not trying to play any games with hiding some. Maybe this had happened to him before. The thought upset Ben who felt like a guilty voyeur on the scene.

Mike pulled out some notes and tossed the wallet back to him. "Now, we could hurt you, couldn't we? But I'm sure you won't even consider reporting this so there should be no need. Just don't let us down."

The man grunted and stepped past him delicately. The youth had left him his plastic. It was almost businesslike. He hurried off to get away from them before they changed their mind about a beating.

"How much we get then?" Mike was talking to himself.

Ben felt a little sick. What if the man really needed the money? He knew all the arguments about having to get by how you could and all the other justifications. He knew that the same people in power who had encouraged his generation to hold money close to their hearts were the ones shocked by the methods of crime that were being employed. However, Ben was no cynic. He wanted what was bright in life, not the sad reality of fighting to get by. They had been lucky. The man was not keen to challenge them, probably made plenty of cash doing something legit. When Ben thought about who else they could have stopped he shuddered. His own father walked this route sometimes.

"Twenty a piece, Ben. See, that wasn't hard, was it? I knew there was nothing to it."

He handed the cash over and Ben stared at the crumpled notes for a few seconds before sliding them into his jeans pocket.

"We could do another one. That would really set us up for the night."

"No fucking way. Let's go down the party. I want this a long way behind me."

Six

The house was rammed by the time they got there and it wasn't yet midnight. Most people would go to a club first and get there about two or three but Ben was concerned that the girl he had joked with in the centre might not hang around if he didn't show till then. From the outside they heard the boom of the system.

"Reminds me of a proper blues party, Ben."

"You never went to a proper blues, boy." He was ribbing him but his feelings towards Mike were confused. He liked the comic side of him, not the face he had seen an hour ago. They had passed by a late off-licence and picked up a small bottle of strong rum and some tins of beer. The cans would go straight to the fridge, probably never to be seen again. This was their contribution to the party drink fund. The rum they would share between them, confident in the effect it would have upon their mood.

The front door was open. Youth spilled out on to the path, the faces slightly flushed with alcohol. They pushed past to the hallway and took in the view. On their right was the living room, which tonight was the dance area. There were about thirty people in there, packed tight. It was mixed and people around their age, but some older guys were sitting round the edges of the room chatting and following the girls' moves to the music. Right ahead of them was the hall leading down to the kitchen and Ben could see a few people talking.

It was loud. Samantha had hired in a proper system and if they had cranked it up, the plaster would have dropped from the roof. As it was he could feel his stomach vibrating with the bass and he started to sway with the beat instantly. Mike went on to the kitchen to find the hostess, leaving him by the group of dancers, pondering on which girl looked the best. As he stood there, smiling occasionally at the single girls, Mike came back up the hallway, followed by Samantha, eager to say hello.

"So, where you been lately? I thought I might have seen you around."

She meant that he should have called in on her or asked her out. He wanted to explain that the pass he made was a drunken error and he was not remotely interested in her but he had to keep the hostess sweet after all.

"This an' that been taking up me time."

She was much shorter than him and he found it hard to see the look on her face but he guessed she was smiling.

"Well you have a good time and maybe we have a little talk later. Have a few things to do back in the kitchen."

"Sure. I be here a while."

She turned back to the kitchen and Ben shot Mike a disgusted look over her shoulder.

"She likes you boy."

"Well me think not, sah."

He had spotted the shy girl from earlier on, sitting on a sofa with two friends. "Watch me now then Mike." He strolled over, head high. "So you come then."

"I was coming anyway. Wasn't you that brought me here."

She was holding her face low with nerves again. He decided to leap in. "So you like the music then?"

"Yeah, course I do."

The DJ was at the far end of the room, crammed in with all his gear. He had just put on a new release that was getting a lot of airplay.

"Well, you dance with me then." He reached down and took her hand.

The two girls next to her were giggling and egging her on and she stood up full of pride. She was quite alluring in tight leggings and a silk blouse that hung low on her bosom. He was surprised by her sudden wave of confidence.

"Hope you know how to dance right boy."

They stepped out onto the dance space. The track was well known and had brought nearly everyone out on the floor. He held her tight by the waist as she twisted her body into a low spiral, set her legs wide apart and began to rub up to him in a slow pulse. As he moved to her side and pressed between her thighs with his leg she responded by dropping her hands low on his back and pulling him into her. Of all the girls on the floor she was the most graceful, no more provocative, but smooth with it. The other couples followed the same path and Ben felt the atmosphere pick up in the room. Another chorus and the beat was a bit louder.

He held her close and began to whisper by her ear. "We can go upstairs for a while. Things I want to do with you."

"Let's just dance for a while. Don't get too rushed with me."

He smiled at her.

"That not too painful I imagine."

After an hour or so the party was buzzing. More people had wandered in from clubs that were closing and every room was heaving. The music still cut across the talk, but from every corner of the place you could hear shouts and cries of laughter. A group of smokers were on the stairs, puffing scented clouds into the dance room and this clouded the dim light even more. Ben stuck with the girl finding Mike now and again for a swig on the rum. It was rough but hit the back of your head with the alcohol swell. He was smoking hard too. The quarter was being slowly burnt but his dance partner was not joining in, saying she wanted a clear head and this made him savour the thought of later on. She was getting heavier with the low grind against him. It was getting harder to move with the tightness of the crowd so they sat down together on the sofa which her friends still perched on. She had to sit on his lap and he positioned her so their bodies met, as if he were inside her.

"Come now. We already waste a lot of time. Let's find some space."

This time she nodded consent, took his hand and let him lead her through the moving throng. They made it to the stairs and pushed past the ranks of youth on each step, finally clearing the top and finding themselves in another hallway. There were still a few people up here, waiting to use the toilet or kissing furtively whilst their partner sought them downstairs. Ben tried a handle and it opened onto a small bedroom. He flicked a light and they saw a small single bed with a pastel blue cover. There were some clothes on the floor, a few paperbacks and a shelf covered in fluffy toy animals.

"Aw, how sweet. Samantha's room."

"Stop it. We can't do anything in here."

It was a feeble protest. He was already slipping his hands up her back, lifting the silk of her blouse.

"Ben . . ."

They were on the bed. He pushed her hard into the

mattress, softly biting her neck and pushing the silk up further. "Cool down before you tear it." She twisted from under him and sat upright on the bed.

For a moment he thought she might leave but she smiled at him and stood up. By the side of the bed there was a small reading lamp and she clicked it on then turned off the main light. It was a much softer tone, the corners of the room were in darkness and the shadows flattered her shape. He pushed himself back to the top of the bed and stretched out, watching her.

She positioned herself in the centre of the room and started to undress. There was no element of sleaze about her actions, she looked at ease and confident, preparing herself. As she slipped the silk over her head he gazed at her breasts, rounded and pert. She wore no bra and they looked smooth and soft in the faint light from the lamp. With a wriggle of her hips she started to slide the lycra from her legs. He knew she wasn't wearing anything underneath—they would have broken the line.

She hesitated for a second as they were just above her hips and then pushed down to show a downy triangle and the sweet curves of her inner thighs, bending slightly so he could see the tiny gap of cleavage between her young breasts. She became a little embarrassed under his gaze and swept at her hair, a blush on her cheeks, then stepped over to the bed.

Ben was still rushed with a girl. He had not learnt the slow delight the body could offer. He was hard and energetic with her. Without touching her sex he loosened his jeans and lifted one of her legs, turning her over and pushing her legs apart. She giggled as she felt him against her leg, crudely trying to mount her and sent soft fingers down to between his legs. She stroked his full length with the tip of her index finger and guided him towards her where she was still moist from dancing with him. He pushed into her in one motion, sliding his arms under her legs and lifting them up so he could push deeper. She let out a low moan and grabbed at her ankles, pulling them back so her legs were almost in a flat open line against his chest. He felt her every movement, felt her breathe. He felt it well up inside him after only a few seconds and came with a series of frantic spasms deep inside her.

They rolled apart after a moment. He had not even kissed her yet and they had finished. His head was spinning from the rum and hash. She was over by the foot of the bed where she had left her clothes in a neat pile and started pulling them on. She was flustered but smiling. Ben felt paralysed in comparison and watched as she finished dressing and reached for the door. He could hear the dull thud of music from downstairs but her whisper cut through it with a roar.

"Boy you come quick, you know."

Curtis pulled up on the other side of the street from the house but could still hear the pounding from the system over the tape he was playing. Amanda was sitting in the passenger seat, one hand on his knee, the other holding a long cigarette. She was wearing a low cut black dress with her hair in a bun to show off her slender neck. The dress was expensive, he could see that, but she was also wearing some crude silver earrings and a necklace that reeked of wealth. On her feet she wore strapless high heels. The only comparison Curtis could make was with a model she looked so good to him, or with women he had seen in the centre of town with oil-tycoon husbands. He felt a mess beside her although he wore a suit, his best. She was wearing a light scent that reminded him of sex. It felt so long ago.

They hadn't spoken much. She had rung him in the early evening and said she was bored. They had seen a dull thriller at an expensive cinema in town and had a quick meal, then he was hoping to take her home but made the mistake of mentioning the party. She said that she saw it as a chance to meet some of his friends, but he suspected it was a stall on the inevitable scene later when he approached the subject of sex. Maybe they could be in and out in twenty minutes.

The party had reached a peak. The front door was slightly open and they stepped through into the mayhem of heaving bodies. Curtis was more aware of the noise and smoke than he would have been had he not had Amanda on his arm. She wakened his senses to anything she may find hard to deal with, but as he looked at her a broad grin broke out on her face and she pulled him into the dancers.

She had no trouble keeping up with the other girls in her movements. Swaying against him, she motioned him to press against her, as if she had something to prove. The low dance thrilled him and he noticed glares of envy from some of the male dancers.

"So Curtis, you finally bring out your new woman for us to meet." It was Ben, racing from the rum and the heat of sex. His face was still flush from the exertion.

"This is Ben, renowned for his subtlety. Ben meet Amanda."

"Charmed indeed."

He was leering slightly but Curtis could understand it. She was oozing sexuality in the dress and he took Ben's interest as a compliment to his luck in finding her.

"Yes, Curtis has mentioned you I think."

"Look Ben, we trying to dance a bit."

Ben was shadowing their moves on the floor, keeping up with them, to talk.

"Me leave you to it then."

He stumbled off into the crowd, thinking of checking the girl again. Amanda hadn't massively impressed him. She seemed a bit square. The thought of the curved partner of earlier was of more interest. His ego had been bruised by her jibe and he wanted a second chance to prove her wrong.

The two dancers were left to concentrate on one another. They pulled tight together and moved low to the bass-heavy groove. As the night grew late the music was settling more, lovers were being given priority. Curtis dropped his hands to her waist and moved them in between her legs. She made no complaint, pushing forwards and opening her legs slightly to aid him and enjoying the brush of his fingers across her thighs and up to her stomach. Amanda was swept up on the wave of the party, the noise and atmosphere. She felt that tonight Curtis would be granted his wish. He was gaining confidence now, still anxious not to offend her but driven by the urge to possess.

He pushed her back away from him, staring at her for a few seconds amongst the throng of bodies. They both understood the pause and turned to the hall, making for the car.

Ben was reaching saturation point. Mike was already crashed in an armchair he had dragged into the kitchen. The rum had defeated him. Ben was not far behind but was keeping his cool. He wouldn't show that he was out of it, despite having consumed vast amounts of hash and alcohol. Wandering through the house, looking for his playmate he kept the firm jaw and set eyes of a sober man. Only when he stumbled against the furniture was it apparent that he was charged.

He searched the rooms carefully but there was no trace of her. Had it been a bit earlier he would have tried to approach another girl but he knew from experience that this was the dead time zone of a party. All the single girls had either met someone or gone home and the remainder were likely to be there with boyfriends. He was in no fit state to take on some jealous buck. Samantha was lurking in the corner of the room with some girlfriends who were staying the night. She looked exhausted but threw him a smile and this made up his mind. Her make-up had deserted her and the prospect of tongue dancing with the battered hostess made his stomach churn. She was violently ugly compared to his conquest of a few hours before. He darted from the room.

He found Mike in the kitchen and shook him out of sleep. The light of the new day had crept up and the room was flooded with an intense yellow glare, making his eyes burn.

"C'mon Mikey. Everyone going."

"Nah, I'll be fine here, just leave me."

"Every party you the same when you get drunk, always come out with the same bullshit about staying." He shoved his hands under Mike's slumped frame and dragged him from the chair. As soon as he found his feet Mike stretched and yawned.

"Fuck man, I have to go to work in about three hours." He stared at his watch with disgust.

"Well I sleeping all day, I tell you."

"Have another drink man. G'wan have a drink with me."

Ben flopped down beside him. "Well, maybe one for the road."

Curtis pushed the door open for her. She stepped through and walked on, into the living room. This time though, she went past the sofa upon which she always sat and made for the bed, easing herself down onto it like a cat. He followed behind her, already pulling at his shirt collar and kicking off his shoes.

"Don't you offer a girl a drink any more?"

It was a reference to the times he had tried to ply

her with wine as a form of seduction. She obviously didn't want to make it too easy for him.

"Of course. It'll have to be gin, that's all I have." He padded over to the kitchen and mixed two drinks. This time he felt no need to give her a huge shot, though it had done no good in the past anyway. She had been brutally frank and pointed out how crude it was to try and get her drunk. This straight element of honesty was one of the chief reasons he found her appealing. She was strong and decided.

When he got back to the room she was between the sheets, her thin dress draped across the bottom of the bed.

"Wasting no time then Amanda?"

"Haven't we wasted enough already?" She lifted her arms to his head and pulled him down to kiss her.

Sending him to get a drink so she could undress was a sign of modesty or embarrassment and to test her he pulled at the sheets to expose her naked body. He wanted everything from her. She held a weak grip on the sheet as he kissed her hard, pulling more until it slipped away and she let out a tiny gasp.

Her body was perfect. His eyes scanned her, seeing no sign of a blemish or mark, only taut, milky skin. Though familiar with her body from the small liberties she had already granted him, the sight of her naked thrilled him. He had never been with a girl so well toned, limbs so slender and proportioned. The evaluation took only a fragment of a second and he dropped his lips to her neck, pushing hard and tasting the sharp flavour of her perfume, his face brushed by her hair. He was still fully clothed and this made him feel powerful.

Many times in the past he had enjoyed sex more when he remained clothed and the girl was naked but Amanda tugged at his shirt buttons and found flesh with her soft touch. He wanted to be naked with her, feel skin to skin.

Expertly she undressed him and now they lay side by side, just barely touching. Her every movement seemed to bring him pleasure, both with her hands and the brush of her leg. As he kissed her brow she slid down his front and nestled her head by his lap. With her hands still caressing him she began to kiss him and then pushed him deep into her, the senses exploding in his head.

The light from the sun was still gaining strength across the sky, bringing life to the endless rows of buildings and factories he could see from the window of his apartment. To the horizon there was the stain of dense housing and industry, no greenery apart from the odd isolated tree struggling in a backyard or patch of waste-land. He stood motionless by the glass panes, studying the East, turning things over in his mind. He was in exile out here. Nobody knew who he was or how to find him. He was just another oddball stranger who had wandered in and stayed, finding security in the anonymity of the place. The only way to gain respect was to be harsh and callous. Here, people fought their way out of a problem and spared no time for the thoughtful. This was their code and he was not part of it, could never be part of it because he could never be so impulsive or fearless. He was a thinker. The things he accomplished came about by spinning thoughts around his mind, finding a path to follow. Zack loved the abstract chase and the way he could implement his thoughts and affect reality with the greedy puppets who were slave to his money. Sometimes though, there were accidents. He felt the mound of the wound on his temple and muttered a curse. Why was he not a fighter? How could he allow a boy to injure him so? That arrogant brat had scarred him and it went further than just the self-loathing caused by the humiliation. The word was spreading amongst the local hoodlums how he had been taken by a kid, a black kid even, and it was not good for his status. Much as he hated the base, animal code here, he had grown used to the set-up and could not change tack now.

After the split with Carl this had been a new territory, somewhere to establish new activity where nobody knew him. He had planned on staying for a year and then clearing out but had never made the money he needed for complete retirement and was now stuck in the middle of the money game. He was more than comfortable, had everything he wanted but could not expand to the point where his investments allowed him to return home and live out his life as he wished. Zack never wanted to work again. He had served his time with the machine and had broken away, first with the Jamaican and then, after betrayal, on his own. It had been he who had set Carl up with his initial capital and watched the money flood in. Those had been good years. After his time as a dutiful member of society watching others make money it had been a joy to reap the rewards of crime. But Carl had become greedy and assembled his own gang. He would never forget the dismissal, the warning. If he went South now, Zack knew the beating he had received from the teenage lieutenant would seem light in comparison with what he would get if he stayed where he was.

Carl would pay for his crime and continued threats.

It had been tough starting here in the East End. He had ploughed his last money into a shipment of powder and crashed it amongst the suppliers. There had been violence, but he had a hired team to handle it and things had settled. His mistake with Curtis had been to underestimate him. The two hired men had been disciplined by their boss for their failure but that was little help for Zack's pride or swollen face. He would have to make sure that Carl's demise would tie-in with some punishment for Curtis, as a fool could see that the young man was a king-killer, hungry for a throne of his own. That humbling could be arranged, maybe even something more severe. What he was setting up was quite flexible and a phone-call to his contact would make sure of his wishes.

He turned from the window and walked over to the kitchen area of the loft. There were no partitions. His bed was in the middle of the room on a small platform and around it lay the trappings of four rooms. The kitchen had all the units and gadgets of a normal home but they stood clustered in a square, stark against the space of the apartment. Next to this pile was a wardrobe and desk with a large mirror. A woman's clothing was resting across the reflective glass and he saw only a fraction of his face as he crossed to the kitchen. He thought he looked old. These rooms were three-sided squares like the scenery in a play. Over on the other side of the bed was a small library and living area. These were walled in by low, black-leather sofas and a long, glass coffee table. This was his office and there was a mess of wiring, snaking round the legs of the furniture, feeding the phone and hi-fi. On either side, sloping windows ran up to the ceiling and the only protection from the flood of daylight were several standing screens of light canvas which Zack would re-position throughout the day should it be too bright. A collection of standing lamps, littered around the huge room, provided light when night fell. All the component parts of the room were white toned. Even the floor was a polished pine, like bone. A soft hum of music rang through the air from wall-mounted speakers. Light, female voices calmed him with a complicated, oriental melody.

Picking up a glass from the floor, he opened the fridge and poured himself some orange juice from a carton. Then he shoved his hand into the freezer compartment and brought out a large tray of ice. He stooped and banged it on the floor. Chunks of it flew everywhere, but some loose ice still in the tray he tipped into his drink, leaving the rest to melt on the wood. He carried the tray over to the bed and sat down slurping at the drink. It had been a long night and he felt dehydrated. The cold hit the back of his throat like the incision of a knife.

"I've made you a drink, darling."

Hidden beneath the thick quilt on his bed was a soft shape and in answer to his voice there was a rustle and a young girl stuck her head out, wiping tired eyes in the bright light. She was lying on her stomach, hugging the pillow.

"Sweet of you Zack."

He swept his hand down the warm curve of her back, balancing the tray on the broad back of his wrist. "But I have a little surprise for you first."

She flashed him a frightened glance through her heavy eyelids, but before she could move he had twisted the tray around and rammed it down between her legs. As she struggled with pain and laughter he pulled one of the cubes free and inserted it deep inside her, pushing with his thumb, holding her tight. She groaned, not sure how it felt or if she was enjoying the sensation, but soon felt the more familiar pressure of him move on top of her, his weight pushing her face into the sheet. He began a slow rhythm into her, whilst slapping the top of her legs, urging her into similar movement. Deep inside her he could feel the cube of ice before it decayed from her heat. He enjoyed the contrast, pushing harder into her still sleepy form, dropping his head to her ear and listening for the tiny rush of air between her lips as he moved.

Curtis and his lover lay together. He could smell sex all over her, the warm, sweet odour of union or lust. It had been both for him. He had at last satiated his desire and had found the depth of his feeling for her alarming. This was far removed from his past encounters, the rough possession of a girl was about all it had ever amounted to. Amanda had given him every aspect of her body, each approach and method she had gone through had given him a tour of her physique and what it offered. Curtis had hardly noticed her dress him with a condom. Slipping it into her mouth and then rolling it along him whilst holding the end tight in her teeth saved the fumbling he had expected. He had known she would insist he wear one and there was an open pack by his bed to save her asking. That was how it was with Amanda. She would not be pressured into sex without protection and this strength again appealed to him. Now they were together and he knew that this was what he'd wanted all along. He had expected his desire to vanish, but he held her tightly in his arms and kissed her softly on the cheek, willing her to hear his thoughts.

Seven

When there was a break in the trees you could see right across the valley, over the bright strip of the river and past the miles of fields and small woods that ran to the horizon. You could see forever in the light of the early afternoon.

Curtis reflected on the winter sun and the way it set everything out with no shadows to blur the perspective. He was lounging in the back of the car as it purred around the perimeter of the park. Amanda was on his mind. They were meeting again tonight. Even though they had slept for only two or three hours, she had left him with her face alive and bright. She'd been late for a meeting with a friend and had had to rush, running around the flat getting dressed. When she had gone he had felt confused but happy, and fell into a light sleep, thinking of her kiss as they had stood at the doorway.

He'd been woken by the phone ringing and Carl's voice growling in his head. The car was outside, Ash driving and the boss taking up most of the back seat even though it was as wide as a sofa. Then to the park, their usual talking place, with the two older men joking about his appearance and obvious activity the night before.

Curtis said little.

He found the best way to get things done was to keep quiet until it mattered and he wanted to find out what was going to be discussed. The park was always private. You could circle the stretch of single-track road, keeping an easy watch on the flat roll of the land around you. Nobody could follow you and there were five exits, so if you knew the roads you could slip in and out at any time you wished. This attention to the detail of his environment was not paranoia but something he had made a habit. Carl had taught him how a man can never be too cautious.

The red and orange hues of autumn were gone, the cold touch of winter had laid bare the trees and even the grass seemed dull and faded. Off in the distance Curtis could see the assorted animals in the small public zoo, about their only companions in the park. It was too early for the trickle of dog-walkers and other visitors to drag themselves from bed.

"We pick you up early 'cause we been up all night. I had a call from them people I mentioned t'you, you remember?" Carl was talking softly and sounded tired with his raspy growl.

Curtis thought of him sipping his brandy through the morning hours and wondered if he was a little drunk. He grunted an affirmative to the question.

"Yes, they want to do some trade and this a big money thing C. Not gonna be piss in your pocket this you know. You have to take a bit more risk to make a lot more money, like I said."

There was a greedy shine in his eyes and he spoke rapidly. Ash drove in silence, listening in and muttering agreement now and again, like a man listening to a sermon.

"You and Ash the men to do it. It easy. You have to be man that all, no' act like some pussyclat pickney like some of the men in the team. An' them grown men C., grown men. Ash here, him not scared, just cautious 'cause him seen gun play, you know? Anyways, you two is gonna make the pick-up. You just give them a case an they give you a case. That easy C?"

"Easy man."

"You follow Ash then."

Now he turned and fished around in his jacket, eventually pulling out a small flask. "Me drinkin' liquor afore you born, Curtis."

They all laughed but Curtis was thoughtful. He was not so keen on taking orders from Ash, which was surely what he had been told to do. Carl would never say so straight to his face, but that was the message. Carl took a long pull from the flask, coughed and put it back without offering. Curtis watched his thick head and the scenery flicking past behind it, trying to work out what Carl had in mind. Maybe this meant Curtis and Ash were his main players now but he found this hard to accept. Carl had never seemed to get on with Ash. He listened as his coughing boss outlined the times and destination. They would leave in the early morning by car and would be back before lunch, the only delay being if the other team failed to show, in which case they were to give them one hour and then leave. There were other minor details about the route and meeting place but Curtis was drifting away in thought. This was big league. When Carl said big money Curtis knew what he meant. All his life he had seen the local players, the money men. He knew how much the car was, bought in cash, the suits and the flat, the trips back to J. Carl was talking tens of thousands of pounds and the thought of money washed over him. The fantasy of buying Amanda silk lingerie and then ripping it to pieces with his teeth mingled with other money dreams. Maybe this would give him the break he needed from Ben and the others who were still running around like kids. Maybe this would give him enough to set up his own thing and make it work. The options rushed through his mind.

"Curtis, you a listen?"

"Yeah, yeah."

"Well look like you a listen then."

They talked the whole thing through. This was going to lift the outfit out of the relative obscurity it had lain in, so they were to be careful. Though the reality of the police was of little interest to Curtis, he knew it would be wise to start playing the game a bit more. No more easy talk with Ben for instance.

"You be carrying from now on remember, just in case. So watch who know it, 'cause that alone get you a year or more."

He didn't want to dwell on the risks of gun play. They were simply there, that was all, just like oxygen was there for you to breathe.

The car circled a small lake and he watched the ducks hiding from the wind at the edge of the water. When he was in the park he could never believe that they were still surrounded by town, ugly brick and stone on every side, just beyond the last row of trees that walled in the green.

He had come here as a child many times. The hostel had had a decrepit van which chugged up the hill to the park once a month, carrying a bunch of excited kids. The memory was pleasant for a few seconds but as always, the thought of those days brought back a darker mood, one he kept buried. It was at the hostel that he had grown hard, silent and had seen the way to progress. There he had learnt that it was better to listen and wait for your moment than to leap in. A set, silent face had earned him respect and he had the strength to back up the image. Curtis had never been given the chance to be a coward. It had been beaten out of him, there was no other way. The experience of those years had hardened him but had also equipped him with a laid-back acceptance of the world that was rare in someone his age. He thought of the others back then and of what they had gone on to do. Curtis envied none of them. His chosen path didn't trouble him.

He flashed back to Carl, coming out of his dream, looking around him to gain his bearings. In a second he recovered and Carl only noticed a flicker cross the face of his apprentice.

Ash was heading for one of the gates. The meeting was over. They would drop him off and the next time he would see them was at the meet. Ash would pick him up first thing, but Carl wouldn't be there. It would be just the two of them and Curtis was not confident of enjoying two or three hours on the motorway in Ash's company.

It would have to be tolerated.

"So, it all straight with you, boy?"

"All straight, Carl."

Eight

Ben stuck his foot out from under the covers to test the warmth of the air. It seemed safe. He had no idea of the time and assumed it was still morning, but drawing back the duvet which was blocking all light as he had it over his head and looking at his watch, he saw that it was nearly half past four in the afternoon. "A ras!"

He was dazed. Trying to remember the events of the night before he thought he could hear his brain tick like a broken machine and lay back in resignation. There had been some drunken arrangement to meet

Mike, he was sure. One of those endless goodbye sessions, with back-slapping and rum-fuelled cordiality. Mike had been in an even worse state. At least Ben had taken a time-out from the alcohol with the bedroom frenzy. He remembered the girl and a twinge of worry struck him. Any reports of his less than perfect performance circulating could be disastrous. He supposed he could always track her down and perhaps improve his record.

The sounds of the street were filtering through to his ears. Tired workers slammed car doors and fumbled with their house keys. Snatches of vague conversation wafted into his room and he recognized the voice of a neighbour. They would all be going to bed in a few hours, he was thinking of breakfast. He was quite happy to slip into the role of the nightfly without feeling guilty. After all, he was in the prime of youth.

He yawned and pushed the covers back a little. The light was a bit too much for his eyes so he flicked the radio on and returned to the gloom of the duvet. From the side of his bed the little tin box pumped out the strains of a current hit and Ben hummed along in a low murmur.

The few minutes since waking were starting to register with him and as the mist cleared from his memory he had to moan. There was a very slim chance that kisses had been exchanged with Samantha on the way out of the house but he couldn't be sure. She had been lurking, that he knew. He tried desperately to remember but the fog was too thick and his head was beginning to throb. Surely he had been too busy looking after Mike, who was stumbling all over the pathway looking for the most inconvenient and unsightly place to throw up, to further embarrass himself with the hostess. It had been clear she was amenable to the idea but Ben's last drunken pass was certainly under the influence of drink. At the time he would have kissed a warthog. The last thing he needed now was some rumour of involvement with Samantha. There were more interesting parties to pursue. He lifted his hands to a throbbing brow and let out a low moan. Samantha could ruin everything with a misplaced word, if she knew the girl anyway. She was bound to.

"Things a lively up down Maxine's lately."

The bark from the radio caught his attention and he pulled back the covers again, forgetting his sore eyes.

"Yes sah! It getting busy at the week's end and that no shock when you check who spinnin' the music, yes, you guess right me have a slot there now myself."

The DJ went on with the usual rant, advertising his night at the club. Ben had thought he might be making a reference to the gun incident but it was just the usual self-promotion. The thought of that night came crashing to his mind and he remembered the girl. She had been the catalyst for his rather foolhardy gallantry and was definitely worth looking up. He had rushed off with Curtis and the girl had slipped his mind what with the strange developments of the last few days. As he slowly ruminated on the recent events of his life, still allowing the music from the radio to pierce his concentration, he remembered her movements on the dance-floor at Maxine's. She had been liquid sex as far as he could recall and the memory provoked a slight arousal in his boxer-clad loins.

The phone started bleeping at the other end of his bed, or was it the alarm? Had he set the alarm because he had to meet Mike somewhere? He couldn't make sense of anything and had to flip his body out of the duvet to shoot an arm out to the receiver. It was definately the phone, as when he picked the handle up there was silence. He looked at it for a second, suddenly feeling a bit drunk after the burst of energy.

Was it wise to attempt conversation in this state?

"Yeah, you talking to Ben."

"Jeez, you talking from the grave, boy. It's Mike, how goes it. Can you talk?"

"Come again?"

"Well, I thought you might have Samantha with you."

"Oh shit."

"You said it boy, she was all over you."

"How the fuck do you know then? You were pissed, Mike, rolling down the fucking road."

"You can't expect me not to notice something like that, can you? Old Sam got her teeth into you, boy."

"Not a word, you hear. Not one word."

"Oh I think she'll take care of that for you. You're in love aren't you?"

Ben could only groan whilst his friend chuckled at the end of the phone. It was obvious that Samantha would waste no time in broadcasting the details of the smooch. Ben only cared because most of his friends thought she was dog ugly. Mike could barely speak now with his laughing.

"I mean looks aren't everything, Ben. You have to

respect a woman for her character these days. I have to approve of your new-man stand on the rights of . . . ugly women."

There was wild hooting now. Even though the hangover was irritating, Ben had to smile. He saw the humour and resisted the urge to accuse Mike of being a virgin to defend his drunken act.

"And I think you had your fun now Mike, so why you ringing?" His head was pounding now. Tablet time had arrived, he realized.

"Why am I ringing? You forgot obviously, that's why I am presently trying to keep your potential customers sweet, though I am suffering with the most vicious hangover and a throat like a crisp."

Another groan from Ben.

"Shit, those guys you were on about, after an ounce."

"Very good Ben, very good . . ."

"Round at your place, four in the daytime we said."

"It's all coming back I presume. Get your ass round here if you want a sale. They might piss off in a minute."

"Yeah, sweet, I'm on my way yeah." He dumped the phone back on the floor and tried to swing his legs off the bed but had to pause to let the room stop spinning. The cramp in his head was getting worse as the poisons of last night began to circulate from their hiding places. *You need the money, you need the money.*

He made it on to his feet and began to assemble some clothes. He had looked better. A silk shirt looked new but his face was crumpled and his trousers felt slightly damp. He picked his jacket off the floor. That at least was unmarked. The colour of the transfer on the back was still a deep red against the black fabric. He nodded approval. He slid his trainers on, glad that fashion did not dictate the feat of tying the laces in his present condition, and checked himself in the mirror. Satisfied that his appearance was sharp enough for the street he made for the door, only to remember that it would be handy to carry some draw with him. Rummaging under the bed he pulled back the carpet where it touched the wall. It was fraying badly. There was a loose board which he prised up and pulled out a green, metal box. The aroma upon opening it was enough to make him feel lightheaded. The sweet tang of good hashish. He had made some small wraps but ignored these and pulled out a ball. If he could persuade Mike's friends to buy an ounce the money from the sale could keep Ben happy for a week. After glancing at the drug and establishing it was one of the preweighed amounts, he wrapped it in some cling-film and dropped it in the inside pocket of his jacket. Before leaving he turned the radio off and checked himself in the mirror one last time.

"There is the face of a small time drug dealer."

He muttered the words with a sigh and straightened his shirt. Every now and again he would make the effort like this to emulate Curtis though he was still only happy in trainers as his footwear. All done he shot out the door.

Mike lived with his parents.

He was an exception to most of his peers in that his mother and father had stayed together in marriage, though it would be too rosy a view to say that all was sweetness and light between them. Indeed, Ben had never been to the house without some outburst or argument breaking out if they were in the same room together. He could never understand how two such incompatible people had come to be a couple. If one of them liked something, then the other was sure to despise it. They were forever opposed. His mother provided the vitriol. She could cut to the bone with her tongue on a bad day. The father would madden her with his indifference. Knowing that this was the one thing guaranteed to annoy her, he would usually glance away or change the subject in a soft whine of a tone at the peak of her anger, thus causing her to turn purple with rage until she started smashing plates as he walked calmly out of the house.

At first, Ben had surmised this to be a weakness in the male and assumed that Mike's mild geekiness was inherited from his father. Maybe his reluctance to leap into bed with girls wasn't just down to his jumbled face but rather his father warning him off women by his own actions. After a few visits though, he could see that the strength was with the father and not with the woman. By infuriating her so and countering this with his placidity, she was perpetually rapt with guilt and Ben suspected that this was a ploy to get the kind of treatment reserved for apologies, including the odd special sexual favour.

He hadn't suggested this to Mike.

Ben had done the same sort of thing in the past himself. One girl he had been with the year before was so insecure after a row that she would do anything to make it up to him. The fun wore off for Ben though. He liked a steady variety of partners and the girl's attempts to keep his interest, despite getting more and more extreme, had proved ineffective. He didn't like hurting girls bodily or emotionally. Ben had always been relaxed in the few relationships he had been in that had lasted for more than two or three weeks. This easy nature in itself would often be enough to wind the girl up. Mike's father obviously relished this tension and kept the marriage permanently on the edge of breakdown.

They were rowing now as Ben arrived but like professionals they broke off to say hello when Mike led him through the hallway. It was one of those dull, council flat hallways, with that brown mottled carpet and cream wallpaper. Mike's parents were framed in battle in the doorway of the lounge, but their heads spun and both smiled hello.

"How's things Ben?"

"Yeah, healthy thanks."

They rushed upstairs leaving the adults to row in the living room. Ben still felt like there was a brick buried in his forehead.

He had tried to run over but had slowed to a walk and Mike was plainly exasperated by his lateness. Ben was not so concerned as he knew the potential smoker would often hang around for hours if he needed some puff.

Mike lived about twenty minutes walk from him. The streets declined from the reasonable appearance of Ben's terrace, down to slummy council stuff by the park and then slowly back up as you got nearer to

Mike's. Ben knew that his father earned more than Mike's and drew some comfort from this when it came to his own status with the parents. There was no glimmer of racism about them, not a trace, and no other white parents had ever struck him this way. It could be that their constant rowing somehow calmed their attitude towards him.

He strode into Mike's bedroom with his chest stuck out and shoulders back. If they were going to buy then it would be at the right price for him—selling large amounts cut his profits down. There were two of them, both with short, rough cropped hair and loose retro-rave look clothing. One of them had a goatee beard and Ben thought he looked ridiculous.

The only space was in the centre of the room. Piles of records covered most of the floor-space, along with a thin bed, still decked with crumpled sheets, and some system equipment. Ben could never understand why Mike had such a powerful set-up as to use it on full volume would surely prompt a visit from the police. As always, it was pumping out the low beat of something current.

"So you have some money for me then?"

One of them pulled out a roll and started fingering it carefully. They were kneeling on the floor and Ben crouched to show them the draw. The washed colour of the banknotes was a glorious sight.

"We want to smoke a bit first."

Ben thought the voice sounded younger than his own.

"You sure you of the age."

They all laughed and Ben broke off a small piece

from the oily lump of resin. Mike was pacing by the windows, nervous at the transaction occurring in his bedroom. The two buyers were not close friends of his and he considered this to be favour for Ben. Though admittedly there was the promise of a few notes as a gesture of thanks as well.

The lads rolled a clumsy joint and lit up, taking deep pulls on it in the attempt to establish their smoking pedigree. Ben was not impressed and started chatting with Mike about the night at the party.

"This is good man. We'll take it if that's an ounce."

He made the transaction, hungrily counting the notes they gave him, then stuffing them deep in his pocket. The two boys split the draw between them then rose from the floor unsteadily and made blank-eyed farewells, saying they would check with Mike if they needed more. They left with Mike showing them to the door. Ben smiled and wondered what he could get up to tonight with his wealth.

"So where you taking me then?" Mike was back at the door, gingerly asking for his reward. He moved around the room cleaning up the mess of the ashtray and opening his window. This allowed him to avoid eye contact with Ben as he wasn't quite courageous enough to demand a cut to his face. They had been friends so long but Ben still failed to understand Mike's awkwardness. He was capable of threatening a complete stranger with violence for cash but was desperate not to offend his friend.

"It alright Mikey boy. I'm gonna get you mashed down at Bliss seeing as the only cure for my ailment is more drink an I figure you in the same boat."

"Safe, Ben. Sounds good to me."

"But you could do me another little help. Remember the girl from the other night, her who was doing the dance round Maxine's?"

"Sure I remember. You mean Celia yeah?"

"Well I don't know her name do I, but I feel I earned the right to buy her a drink or two when I made that stand. So chase her up an see if she can meet with we tonight. You can introduce us properly." The hangover was deserting him. Having some money had proved an elixir for his ache and he circled the room with a slight swagger.

"You getting a bit busy aren't you? What about the girl from the party, she was criss man."

"Chaa, girl from the party can wait. The way things have been going lately I have to research every option and see what turn up positive in the laboratory."

Mike was laughing as Ben adopted a mad professor tone to his voice. "I'll see if I can chase her up then. Now, what you doing?"

"I think it might be bath time for Benny. Ring me later yeah?"

They walked out of the room to the top of the stairs where the strains of the fighting downstairs was audible. Mike was oblivious to it, having spent most of his life with his parents rows in the background, he now took it for granted.

"This aggravation is gonna give you problems in later life you know, Mike."

"Nah, just means I can play my music as loud as I want."

Nine

The highstreet was trying hard to look appealing in the winter dark. All the shop windows were lit brightly to persuade the potential shopper that they were still open. It was just after six and Mike had set out to find Celia. He was going to the tiny boutique where she worked and it was near the record store he laboured in. He had to drop by there anyway to find out his hours for the following week. This is what he told himself but he could simply have phoned. His motive was really to help Ben as usual and show him that he did know the girl. The truth was that they had only spoken a few times and she had never been particularly chatty. He wasn't quite sure how he would handle the invitation on behalf of his friend and walked slowly, half hoping she had the day off or had left early.

The street was the normal collection of chain shops and take-aways with a local shop every few hundred yards. It was busy he thought and people were already gathering in the local bars, trying to block out the cold with a quick brandy before home. Weaving through the traffic he crossed over to the alley where Bliss was hidden and walked through to a small cluster of shops set back from the highstreet. The lights were still on in her shop and without pausing he pushed through the door and past the rails of clothing.

She was staring at him from behind the cash desk, surprised at the late customer until a faint sign of recognition crossed her face. He was struck by her looks. The environment made no difference, even in this dusty store she looked beautiful. The light made it hard for him to focus on her without an obvious stare but her face was framed by thick, jet hair setting the skin against the perfect frame.

"Mike, from the record shop."

Relief relaxed her features. He must have looked jumpy when he approached her.

"Oh yeah, I remember. You were down the club the other night weren't you. Sorry, got a terrible memory for faces and names."

The voice didn't quite fit the mystery of her face. It was the familiar drawl of the area.

"Yeah that's why I came in actually."

He bobbed his chin up and down with nerves and

she smiled. It struck him that she was maybe some years older.

"Remember the guy who walked over and straightened out . . ."

"Yeah we had a word didn't we? I was going to talk to the police an' everything but the club doormen told me not to bother with it but I was a bit wound up, you know? What? You a friend of his then?"

She was chatty. He felt a bit more relaxed. It wasn't that he was nervous talking to girls, he found it easy. But the messenger task made him feel awkward.

"Well we're going for a drink tonight. Thought you might like to come an say hello."

"Course. Me no do anything tonight."

She was moving from behind the desk and Mike couldn't prevent himself from following the sway of her hips with his eyes. Dancing was not required for her to proclaim her sexuality. Her lithe frame shifted in smooth movement, each limb complementing the other. She was in lycra again, emphasising the roll of her body.

Stepping right up to him she smiled and tilted her head back a little, showing the depth of her neck. Mike could see she was adept at presenting her body for scrutiny.

"Where you a go and I come down to buy him a drink."

"Just round at Bliss."

"Fine, then I see you there."

Was she coming on to him? Surely she was moving closer so her breast was almost stroking his chest. He could smell the light musk of her fragrance. Mike had never been with a woman. He imagined dragging her into the back of the shop and letting her abuse his body but a bolt of fear smothered his dreaming. He backed away slightly and noticed the smile curl across her lips like she had tasted something sweet.

"Yeah, we'll see you there then."

She was waving goodbye as he shuffled backwards to the door and fumbled with the handle, a coy grin on her face. Once out he breathed deep and hurried round the corner.

In his nightly fantasies Mike would regularly make it with black girls. In fact, it was more often a black girl than white. He was usually strolling down a beach or through a warm glade somewhere and would come across some lightly clad, desperate girl who melted under his gaze. The dream would get more cloudy after this point as he wasn't exactly sure what would occur but he had a fairly good idea from the more graphic videos he had watched. It generally ended with him panting across a heaving bosom which was an image of special appeal for him.

Mike was growing concerned at his failure to leap into bed with someone. He tried to follow Ben's example but lacked the daring streak required for an initial conquest. Ben was getting a bit out of control in Mike's eyes anyway.

He was pushing past the shoppers again, lost in thought above the grinding of gears and rumble of engines from the stream of traffic. Music blared from open shop fronts, defying the cold, to try and draw the shopper in. Six months ago he would have been in a large group of youth at this time of day. They would have hung around a few food bars, laughed at the girls and maybe chased off some unwelcome visitors from a neighbouring school. Though their pursuits in the evening had grown more mature over their last few years of study, to include drinking and in some cases regular girlfriends, the street was always where they felt comfortable. A burst of youth on the street. Now most of them had either taken jobs, gone off to study in town or were turning to more immediate ways of getting ahead. Mike could have studied. He was bright enough and his teachers had tried to persuade him to go for a place at a college but Mike hadn't been interested. He saw no advancement in study as he knew exactly what he wanted. Getting it was another matter.

Mike needed a little money to set up a small music store and to get away from the grouchy bastard he worked for now. At least the job was roughly along the lines of what he wanted to do though. He had seen people's expectations soar from watching his parents. Much of their frustration came from their own idea of what they should have in the material sense. Mike was not going to fall into the same trap. He would get a shop by whatever means and would then be happy, he was sure. The mugging had been so easy. He was big enough to intimidate the victim and had no qualms about dealing out a few blows should there be some reluctance to hand over the cash. The years of hassle from his peers had taught Mike how to hurt someone if it was needed. Very occasionally he imagined beating the crap out of Ben, to turn the tables one day, but knew that Ben did not intentionally abuse his nature and it was really his own fault. Still, he was confident he could defeat him. Ben was floating at the moment he thought. He had always been a lazy character and was not cut out for study but at the same time was quite incapable of making any serious money in lawless ways. He was too slack and had some sentimental principles. The mugging had shown this. Mike started to work out how much he could earn from a steady operation as he paced the miserable highstreet. The figures were good. If he made forty or round that a time then he could pull in two grand a week almost. He began to dream of a steady wage from it, lost in a trance.

He was crossing the street now at a set of lights, deep in mathematical computation when a car sounded its horn. Thinking the noise was an insult Mike reared up to scream back some abuse. It was Curtis, laughing at his scowl. Mike jogged over to the side of the car.

"Want a spin back to your yard, Mike?"

Curtis was dressed as impeccably as ever. Today he had gone for the full suit and was looking sharp. He had even taken the car to the wash so the black sheen of the bonnet reflected the tiny lights of the night flying past. This evening he was taking Amanda for dinner in town and wanted everything to be perfect. He was still feeling up from the night they had spent together and had been dwelling on his imminent financial boost after the deal coming up. He was a little annoyed he couldn't mention it to Mike as he knew he would have lapped up every word. Today he even had time for Mike.

"So what new then, Mike? Didn't really get a chance to talk when I last saw you."

Mike had guessed that Curtis had a problem hanging with a white guy these days and was less willing to play the impressed schoolkid routine than he had been in the past. Curtis wanted some acknowledgment for his fearlessness at the club, but Mike had never been as respectful of Curtis as he was of Ben. He saw Curtis as an equal. This was partly because he knew that Curtis could take more sophisticated criticism and humour than Ben but also because they had once been close, before Curtis fully resigned himself to the gangster life.

"Oh just the usual, nothing exciting."

By ignoring any reference to the fight he made Curtis realize his mistake. It was easy to take Mike for a fool like Ben did.

"Me seeing a girl regular now, you know."

"Yeah, I saw her at the party."

"Oh you was there?"

"In the kitchen most of the time."

He was driving fast, rushing round to Mike's house. Being unable to brag about his coming task meant Mike was rather dull company. There was little to discuss.

As they turned a corner he had to brake hard to avoid a stationary car. They were away from the high-street now, in the middle of the complex of residential streets where Mike lived. Lights were on in the houses, flickering television screens lighting up the scrawny row of low trees that lined the edge of the pavement. Curtis had dressed and left his flat only twenty minutes before. Dropping Mike off would make him five minutes late as it was and the parked car was not helping. He should never have given him a lift. Now he was stuck in the backstreets.

He blew the horn and they both stared at the car in front waiting for some movement. The road had parked cars on either side and there was only room for single lane traffic but the driver was not waiting for someone to pass. The road ahead was empty. He was just sitting there.

"What this guy doing?"

He leaned on the horn. The long, metal scream of it was a shock for the rows of terraces. Lights came on in the house to their left and two men came out into the pathway. As they shuffled out, the door of the car swung open and a fat man in his forties turned to look at them.

Curtis would have left it. He had no need for the hassle or being late for Amanda, but Mike had something to prove. He hopped out of the passenger door and rose up to his full height in the middle of the street. The movement surprised Curtis. Mike was not renowned for throwing himself into trouble though Curtis knew he was no coward.

"So you gonna move the fucking car then?"

The men in the driveway came down to the edge of the street. They had blank faces, as though waiting for the other man to react. He slammed his door and turned to Mike.

"You're a bit pushy ain't you son? What's your problem?"

"Got somewhere to go haven't I. So move it."

The man turned back to his car, opened the door and reached inside. When he pulled his bulk back out he had a short metal tube gripped in his fist. Mike appeared undaunted.

"Doing something then are you?"

Curtis sat behind the wheel and sighed. He would have driven off but he couldn't leave Mike on his own in the street and he had a suspicion that this gesture was on his behalf. The three men couldn't see through the smoked glass of his car so this couldn't be a racial thing. He wondered if Mike knew this. He clambered out of his side of the car.

As soon as they saw him the atmosphere changed. Maybe they would belt Mike about a bit, but they wouldn't hurt him too bad for being impudent. But now Curtis noticed the cold wave of hate that swept over their faces as he moved to the back of the car. The two by the pavement became animated. There was a point to this for them now and not just slapping a jumpy motorist. This bastard was acting high and mighty with the horn.

"Think you own the fucking road, don't you?" It was a snarl of a voice, thin and menacing. They looked past Mike towards the real target for their coming aggression. "In a suit an all."

They laughed the slow, ugly taunt of the street. Now Curtis was getting angry. He could smell their ignorance. Mike had instigated this but was a side-show now. The three in front of him advanced slowly, the fat man brandishing the metal rod.

Curtis flicked the boot up. They knew he was going for something, maybe even glad that there would be more of a contest than just kicking him down. He pulled back from the car, slightly hidden by the boot and stepped out a few yards behind Mike.

His friend was confident of the respect that Curtis could earn with a glance but he saw horror spread across the features of the attackers. He stood firm, watching them shrink back with a puzzled smile on his face.

"What, the odds too hard on you then?" Curtis brushed past him, slowly going up the street towards them as they retreated at the same pace. The fat man dropped his weapon.

"No need for that now is there? I mean nothing happened, right?"

"Move the fucking car then." Curtis sounded relaxed, in control. In his right hand Mike could see the dark metal of the gun. He had it lowered, pointing at the floor. The fat man leapt into the driving seat, called the engine to life and tore off up the street. The others disappeared into the house. Mike could hear the key turn in the lock.

Simply witnessing all this he felt the buzz of power. There was nothing for the men to do against the threat except retreat. He stared on at the now empty street until Curtis called him. He was back in the car, leaning out of Mike's window.

"Move your ass, Mike. I'm in a hurry you know."

They pulled off at speed. Curtis had the lights off, thinking that if they decided to take the model and number it would be harder to spot. He knew there was little to worry about. If he got a pull now then it would be a simple puzzle to figure out who had done the dialling. They would be too scared to call the police, there was always the risk he would return.

The streets flew past under the darkening sky. There was some light left in the West and it gave the clouds an ugly edge, as though a storm was gathering.

"That was dumb, Mike. Let me tell you one thing. If you going to be big then do it with the right people at the right time. Fatso there would have moved the car anyway."

"Thought you always said that you had to stand up, never give an inch, all that crap if you want some respect."

"That true, but in moderation."

"You pulled a gun. That's a funny moderation in my book."

"It was the quickest way out of the situation, anyway . . ." There was nowhere to take the conversation with Mike, he seemed too headstrong. Curtis still felt that he had made the stand for his benefit but decided not to push the point. He had never seen this side of Mike before.

They pulled up by his house.

"So what you do tonight, anyway?"

"Oh, think I'm gonna see Ben and some girl. Out for a drink at Bliss."

"You boys drink it up these days, don't you?"

"Nah. Can't afford to." Mike felt like he did talking to his father. There was no validity to the words.

"Anyway, I catch you later then, Mike."

Mike walked slowly up the path to his door, spinning round to see the black shape of the car take a corner and vanish from his sight.

"Arrogant, thankless bastard," he muttered, and turned back to the door.

Zack checked the line of his trouser-leg was straight and then sat back into the smooth comfort of the leather. At his side was a small table with his drink and a steel ashtray. His cigarette was burning away, balanced on the metal rim. He stared at the girl in the chair opposite. The black hide engulfed her, making her look quite juvenile in her dark dress, her legs drawn up underneath her.

"That's for the whole two days darling, remember."

"How could I forget?"

He leaned forward again and picked up his wallet from the central coffee table that separated them. Moving closer to her allowed him to catch the scent she wore and for a second he thought of having her for another day. She was bright and interpreted his hesitation.

"Please Zack, I am in a bit of a rush."

Such elegant vowels for a girl who made people pay. Thinking of the things they had done and how he had instructed her to respond made him smile at her apparent sophistication now. She looked uneasy. It must be the figure who waited by the glass of the windows, the man who had arrived whilst she was still dressing and had enjoyed the sight of her flesh as she rapidly covered it.

"You always retain your grace, my sweet. Here you are." He handed her a slip of paper from the wallet and she hid it in her dress with a ripple of her fingers.

Then she lifted herself out of the chair and rose to her full height. She was thin but very tall and the dress hung from her to expose the assets of her figure. Letting him savour the sight for a few seconds, like the skilled temptress she was, her confidence returned and she flashed him a wide smile, whilst starting to move for the door.

"I expect to see you again in the near future. Until then . . ."

All the time he watched her from the sofa, studying her form. As she approached the door the other man moved out of the darkness and positioned himself in front of her. His movement was silent, like he was on rails. He seemed to blend with the shadows. "Let me have the pleasure." His voice was raspy, full of lust.

Though she could see little of his face in the dark, the voice told her of his desire. He was tall. She had to step back to stare up at him. He was a client she would never accept, as after a year or two in the play, she had learnt how to spot the danger signs in men and what they would expect of her. Zack was the limit of what she would do and he never really hurt her. Sometimes he would even come close to satisfying her desire. This man though, looked twisted enough to really damage a girl. She was glad that this was her departure and not the start of her work and that she still picked her own customers from a select few, she was good looking enough to do so.

"My you really are sweet you know." He brushed her cheek with the back of his hand. It was rough enough to hurt. She could smell alcohol on him and cheap perfume. The accent made her shiver, it was so clear what he wanted just from the tone.

"The door was mentioned, your pleasure I think."

He chuckled and opened the wide block of wood behind him, just enough for her to have to squeeze past him, brushing against him with her breast. She pushed past and pulled the door tight but still he did not change his stare. Even though she had gone he preserved the moment, looking at where she had been. They heard her footsteps rushing down the iron stairway.

"You shouldn't scare a girl like that, Ash. She's too young for that sort of thing."

"She not too young for anything, when she do it for money." He was moving down to the living area where Zack still basked on the wide leather sofa and then turned to the wall of windows. His height allowed him to peer down into the yard that Zack's building towered up from and he watched the girl jump into a small sports car and pull away. "All the help you getting from me I think I need a little reward. Few hours with her would be sweet."

Zack spoke to his back. "I'm afraid she's fussy, Ash. She snares you, making you think she might be giving it away, gives you a sample and then before you know it you're paying by the night."

"Not me sah. I get the sample then after that she want nothing else!"

"Anyway. I think there is another reason why you are here, is there not? Other than leering after the girl, that is."

"The girl special man. You fix it up for me." He

moved to the sofa like a cat, so that Zack noticed the liquid nature of his body movements.

Ash was quiet on his feet, a dangerous man. He fell back into the chair the girl had been sitting in and a hard edge came to his face as he started to think of the business that had brought him here. To Ash, pleasure and work were two separate things, but each was to be taken as seriously as the other. He would have the girl but that would come later. "All set Zack. We go in the morning."

"The money?"

"Every last dollar him ave, I tell you. I fix it all, I told you. Even got Curtis going as my watcher. The one who do you the other day."

Zack needed no reminding. He had been confined to the loft, nursing his wounds. It would not be wise to go out and be seen with a bruised face, that was why he had summoned Marian. She was good at distracting him. He had mentioned Curtis to Ash and was pleased that the young man was going along on the trip.

"I want him hurt rather badly, Ash."

"No a fear'd of that, sah. Any man who there wid me going to be hurt if these yard boys are what you say they are."

"Don't worry. They just want the money. I break Carl and you step in, everybody happy."

"Yes, an he who lick you down get slapped. That please you, I feel."

Zack noticed how Ash could change his tone from being subservient to being quite arrogant. It was a sign to him how erratic this man was. When he had first called him in to suggest the idea, Ash had been childishly excited. Zack knew a team who would pose as potential allies, then pull the cross and take the blame. Carl would be weak and broke and would fall to the take-over from Ash, the man who would then pair up with Zack to control half the town.

Curtis would be punished along the way.

However, this evening Ash was sounding brash and cocky, a bad partner. Maybe the girl had triggered some bravado in him but Zack was not pleased by the reference to Curtis. His mind started to ponder the plan and other avenues it could take.

"Just make sure you don't blow it, Ash. I want no fuck-up, you understand?"

"No fuck-up, Zack. Now pour me a drink rasta, I beg you. Girl make me thirsty."

Ten

He was the only black guy in the restaurant but this did not concern him. He had the class superlative, a fat wallet. Anyway, he was not the only exception—she was the best looking girl—she was smoking, twisting the cigarette around her fingers. He stared at it, thinking it might snap at any second under her caress. The few extra years she had on him had given her the brush of womanhood and any hint of girlishness had been transformed into an adult awareness of her sex.

When he picked her up at the flat she was dressed to go but he gave in to the urge to have her at once.

She had answered the door with a look of pure desire and he abandoned the placid mood he normally tried to adopt and pushed her back into the room, spun her round and positioned her across a chair. Within seconds he was inside her and took her roughly, proving to her how base he could feel about her. She encouraged him with little sounds of pleasure and arched lower when he came in her.

In the car she kept her hand low on his crotch. She had changed into the black dress she now wore as he had pulled the other out of shape back at the flat and he could slide his fingers deep between her thighs. They had talked about cancelling the restaurant and going to bed but Amanda had wanted to go out. This was typical of her. Even though she wanted him as much as he wanted her she felt guilty not fulfilling the other actions of the evening. In any other girl Curtis would have found this maddening and just kept her at the flat or walked out but in Amanda he loved this strength. Her determination with even these petty things intrigued him.

Now they just stared at one another, smiling.

"I've got something big on tomorrow. Have to go out of town." He wanted to tell her about the transaction but could only tantalize her.

At once her eyes lit up from the slightly dopey glimmer the sex had caused. "So. Pulling off a big deal are you, Curtis?" Her tone was provocative, trying to sound childlike but he knew the sarcasm was to get him to disclose some details and laughed. "I can't tell you everything, now can I? But yeah, it big. And when it finish, I'm going to treat you to a holiday."

Curtis had never been out of the country, never really thought about it but thought the idea of travel would appeal to Amanda.

"Oh! Going to take me somewhere exotic then are you? Like where?"

"Maybe over to America I was thinking."

"You like to rush into things a bit don't you. We've only been together a few days."

"Only bodily. In mind we been together for a long time."

She laughed and studied the menu and when she had found the most expensive dish, sat back and thought about the meal her gangster man was going to buy her and what she would give him in return. Curtis was going to be a happy youth. In his mind things were really working out for him.

Where was Mike? He had rung and said eight was the time to meet but Ben had only turned up at half past the hour and there was no sign of his friend or the girl. He saw Adam and Petie and strolled over. They were at a booth, clutching bottled beer. Adam nodded hello as he stepped up to the table. Ben hadn't seen him since the tip for selling hash to Paul over in Sheltham and he was reminded of Astrid and her kiss. It seemed months ago but in reality it was only a few days. Maybe he had been a bit too busy lately.

"Easy there, Ben. How things treat you?"

"Can' say fair."

Adam was the talker. These two were like glue together.

"So, you earnin' alright?"

"Await. You know what I a do. Was you that send me to that kwashi over Sheltham."

"Oh, I sorry. Him a fool I know. I sorry 'bout that if it no work out." He grinned and turned to Petie. Obviously it was no big surprise that Paul had been a jerk. Adam liked playing little jokes on people. It made him feel on top. Petie grunted and took a swig of beer. He was on hand to make sure Adam was never bothered. Ben was smiling about it now but had he wanted to be angry, Petie had the gift of being able to calm people down. Usually with a few heavy blows to the head.

These pair ran a car parts order chain. Someone wanted a mirror or a rad' and they could get it in twenty-four hours through Adam. They didn't limit themselves to profits from selling though. Adam was a sharp, ratty thinker and he made loans with his money. Not really a shark, more like an unofficial banking service, he generally knew everyone's status financially and would sidle up to you if he knew you were short—under the shadow of Petie of course.

Ben had been approached many a time but was not dumb enough to take a loan. If he needed money that badly he could check Curtis. "I take it you two still in the same line of work?"

"That the case yeah."

"So, you see Mike?"

"You still hanging with that dick? No, me no see him."

Adam was usually in Bliss. It was the centre of his operations. If a customer needed him then he could be sure of finding him there, slumped in a booth with Petie by his side.

"Well, I take off then. Take it easy."

"Safe, Ben."

He moved over to the bar and dropped onto a stool. That was a bit worrying. Adam knew he was selling so the boys who worked here surely would and they would not be happy about it. This hadn't entered his thinking before. Ben only worried about things when they happened. He had seen a few scenes here in the past over draw and didn't want to appear in one himself.

The place was filling up even though it was early. There were some couples dressed up, the younger ones in street-wear jeans and slick tops and a few in suits. The place was bright and noisy, sound bouncing round the walls from the hi-fi and the conversation growing louder with the arrival of more people and the flow of alcohol. West Park was no slum, though it had rough areas. There was money here and it was nothing to spend fifty on a night out. He was glad he had the roll from the sale that afternoon and ordered a white rum from the barmaid. She was sassy-looking in a tight, white blouse and high skirt and he watched her cruise up and down the bar. Ben had the female shape on his mind. There was nothing else worth concentrating on at the moment and the last few days had seen a few notable sessions. Tongue batting Samantha sent a shiver down his spine and he flashed back to reality.

He was getting glances from a table of girls off to his left and he caught sight of himself in the bar mirror to check his look. He wore a two piece outfit of a bright yellow. It was a soft yellow cotton, almost African looking but cut in a style way. His hair was short and tight and tonight he had donned his one item of jewellery, a thin gold chain with a sovereign set in it. He admired himself.

"So, my knight size himself up then? Don't you think you pretty enough for me?"

The girl's voice came from behind him over his shoulder and he flicked his head round to counter her with a comment on the way she looked herself, sure he could find some defect and begin the flirt.

He was silenced by the face of the very girl he awaited.

Celia gave him a catty smile. She was everything he remembered but up close he felt the rekindling of the lust he had felt for her at the club and was relieved that the drink and draw had not flattered her. The skin was perfect, a very light shade, almost a redskin, and the hair was set up in a thick jet style setting off the shape of her cheek and jaw. Compared to the girl from the party and the shy prettiness that had attracted him, this girl was cast in heaven. She was dressed plainly but it accentuated her figure. A long white top, looking like it had been sprayed on with an aerosol and tight cream leggings brought out her shape. She wore some rounded leather shoes that were more a straight look but they suited her posture which was slightly official, office like.

"Well, what you think?" He pushed his hand back through his hair and stepped off the stool. She was taller than him and he had to stretch to be the same height.

"T'allright. Where your friend then?"

"Soon come. Don't worry about him though, he just the messenger boy. Was me who wanna see you."

"I thought so. Well you better take me out then. There a dance over in Bridge End I was going to, if you want. I meet a girlfriend over there," she rested on the bar, talking easily.

He watched her lips move, thinking about the potential of the night. Where was Mike? He might be an essential diversion later.

"Bridge End far though. We could just go Maxine's."

Speaking to her he felt like it was all arranged. There was no mention of the conflict at the club, they were just discussing spending the night somewhere. This was easy. Ben was already undressing her in his mind.

"No. I want to dance a bit and I go Maxine's all the time. So you want to come or not?" She shot him a smile, knowing full well that he was snared.

"Whatever you say girl, I be there."

Mike was on a street running from the highroad. He hugged the shadows of a garage door, bracing himself against the cold. Time was running out. Ben might dig up if he had to wait, it depended on the girl. He had decided he couldn't sponge off his friend all night and had come out to this dark spot to roll someone for his night's spend. It was not just the money, though that was how he rationalized it to himself. He had got a rush from the last time and it had been so easy. Curtis was in a different league to him these days, and he had felt humbled by the scene with the gun. When he had first stepped out of the car, Curtis had been worried. Mike had been on top. Producing the gun though was a snub almost. What could he do to back that up?

Treated like a jerk by most people, Mike had felt in control with the violence of the previous mugging. Ben had been scared. It was the only time he had felt superior to him and his casual angle on life and he knew that turning up with a wad would impress his friend. He sighed. Twenty minutes had passed and only some old bat walking her dog had passed him. It was cold. He was only wearing light denims and his feet felt like they would snap off if he moved. In the pocket of his denim jacket he fingered the glassy edge of a knife handle. An old lock-knife he had bought years ago on a disastrous family holiday to Spain. His father had helped him choose it. He smiled at the memory. If he could see him now.

There was a sound down the street. This part of the patch had thin clusters of terraces with lots of corners, as the streets were packed in tightly. They were probably where the better-off factory workers had lived in the days when everyone had a job. The sound bounced down the pavement coming towards him. They were heavy footsteps, not too promising. He was not a coward but it would be foolish to tackle someone who looked serious, even with the knife. The thought of Bliss danced round his mind. That, and un-rolling a pack of twenties at the bar.

"Got a light mate?"

The man stopped. He was only in his twenties, shoulder length hair and a soft face dressed in a heavy overcoat that hid his shape. He thought back on how a friend of his had told him to check for any scar tissue and drop out if there was any but this guy was baby smooth. Baby-face was also a good deal shorter than himself so Mike decided to take the risk. He felt oddly calm, as though this was set out for him like a vocation. Pushing forward as the man looked up in alarm, he slapped him across the face to stun him, then shifted his tall frame around to his back and pushed the edge of the knife into the overcoat, just to let him feel it.

"Yeah, yeah what is it? Whatever you want."

"I want your money of course, you dumb fuck, give it, now!"

The figure twisted to let his hands drop to his pocket and pulled out a dark wallet. "That's it. Everything. I swear."

Mike pushed him away and peered down at the money. There was a solitary fiver nestling in between the walls of the purse.

"That it?"

"Times are hard, pal." The man was not from round here. His accent branded him a country boy.

"There must be more. What you doing for tonight?"

He had let go of him but the man stood his ground to answer. "Watching the TV now I suppose, can I have the wallet? It was a present from my girlfriend."

"Give her my love." Mike tossed him the gift and paced off.

He sat at the bar in the same seat Ben had an hour before. His friend had left though, leaving a note with the barmaid telling him about Bridge End and the girlfriend who might be there waiting for him. No problem on a fiver! Bliss was packed now. Full of people out to spend money. Spending on a girl or just getting smashed to forget about a bad day. The music was loud. A tune Mike knew well was pumping, the DJ mouthing off about his girl action in a bass drawl and Mike watched as the local girls swept from table to table letting the guys size them up.

He turned back to the bar and ordered a beer. A fiver. One bullshit fiver. The forty must have been beginner's luck, but it did make sense. For that amount it was worth the effort. Why was he on the street trying to grab the stuff when there was so much floating around? Looking round Bliss you could see plenty of money, most of it gathered in ways not wildly different from his own, he imagined. It was easy work as well. The guy had been all too willing to hand over.

"This note's bent."

"You what?"

"It's bent, dud, not kosher, boy."

The barmaid had dragged the manager over. He reached over and took the pint glass out of Mike's hand.

"I know you must have got it somewhere legit but my advice is take it back and get a refund."

"At least let me have the pint."

"No way."

This was too much. A mugger being stitched.

"Need a float Mikey boy?"

"Hello Adam."

*

The only concern Ben had at that moment was trying not to get too excited. The girl was rubbing up against him so smoothly and with such regular strokes that it was surely on her mind to embarrass him with a liquid outburst. Ben felt like he could blow steam.

He had never been to this club. It was a good thing Mike had not shown because this was a straight black venue. He couldn't see one white face. The music was heavy, drifting into slow reggae stuff from time to time but mostly the minimal pulse of ragga. She was bringing it to life. The thin accent of the guitar, the bass rumble and tin hi-hat squeak—she brought out every rhythm. Most of the songs she was the essence of what they were talking about. She was sex on him. She had pulled off the top and wore a tiny cover for her breasts which just about hid her nipples but then encouraged him to seek them out now and again, when she turned and let him push into her from behind. It was dark and Ben could only make out the shapes of the other couples, moving on the floor. The music filled his head, drove his body low to the floor, locked against her. So far she had not let him kiss her as she wanted the suggestion to arouse him on its own and her plan was working. Ben was a happy player in her hands. He could feel a thin layer of moisture on her arms and stomach when they touched and wanted to taste the sweat, push her legs apart and drive into her. He knew the girl could go for hours with the tease. For some it was more pleasure than the act itself, like a woman enjoying foreplay forever. There was a break in the music and he pulled her off toward the side.

"You want a drink, girl?"

"Vodka and tonic with a lot of ice."

Though she spoke strongly he could hear a hint of worry in her voice. He had spoken quite harshly, as though he was a little bored and had surprised her with the tone. He turned away from her and made for the bar which was up a small flight of steps. She stared after him a little puzzled and then went back to her dancing. She didn't dance so wild as she had before.

He found the bar and ordered her drink and the same for himself. It was expensive but he had the roll and anyway, girls got in free so that gave him twice as much to spend, in theory. Looking around he saw he was young for the club. The bar was full of men a good ten to fifteen years older than himself, dressed up, so he looked pretty cheap as they had some real money to spend. He was thinking of later, where to take her. There had been no girlfriend and he guessed this was a plan to get him out to the club but she needn't have worried. He would have followed her to Poland. The important thing now was not to spend all night here dancing. Ben had already reached the stage where he wanted her badly and he had to admit the money wouldn't last forever. The taxi over had been twelve, the drinks would soon add up. If he acted a bit disinterested he might be able to speed things up a bit.

When he got back to the floor she tried to pull him back to her to continue dancing but he held off and motioned to some seats. The place was low-ceilinged and the seats were on a platform, so their heads were only a foot away from the roof.

"This a funny place, you know."

"Why that?"

"It all old men up in the bar, but the girl pickney."

"That what you think of me?"

She was angry, he could tell from the voice. Her attempt to conceal it was a good sign as it meant she was sensitive to his reaction.

"Well I don't know yet do I." He shot her a look telling her what he wanted and drained his glass, banging it on the table.

"You rush a girl a bit."

"Rush to the good things, yes. Where we gonna go?"

She decided the best way to fight his eagerness was to shock him and she adopted a cold tone to her voice. She was surprised at how much she liked him, but it was just a physical thing. He was a bit too easy-going to interest her any other way.

"Well I better get back to mine anyway, if you wanna dig up."

Ben winced. She must have thought he had meant he wanted to crash. This was not what had been intended but it was too late, she was rising to leave.

When the cab pulled up on the highstreet Ben fished in his pocket for the fare and she jumped out without waiting. A thin rain coated the street in a shiny veneer and it reflected the few lights still burning. He could just see her move up a side street and vanish from sight. The driver was slow with the change. Ben had been too teased to give up now, so, charged with the alcohol and his desire for her he decided to give up the money, leapt out of the cab and ran up the street she had taken.

She had gone.

There was a long line of blank terraces and their shoddy hedges ran up a hill into the distance. Lines of cheap cars ran up either side and he began walking up the street between them, checking the porches. This was not good. The rain was already dripping from his brow and his feet were sodden, each step producing a noisy squelch. It was nearly two in the morning and it would take him a while to walk back to his yard. He had given the driver the last of his money.

He turned round and began to walk back to the main road. Going up the hill was not going to help.

"Ben, boy. Come in from the rain."

She let him in the half open door and led him up the stairs. The house smelt musty like yellowing newspaper and not one light was on.

"My mother sleep next to my room so you can't make a sound, right."

He nodded and followed her into a tiny room at the front of the house where she went to the side of her thin bed, leaving him to stare out at the street. She must have been watching him as he paced up and down looking for her, finally taking pity. She turned a light on by the bed and he saw how small the room was. A chest of drawers and small wardrobe were crammed in by the wall and where he stood was the only free space big enough to stand in. There was no clutter of screwed up clothes or anything on the floor, and the room was bare apart from some posters on one wall, she must keep everything packed away he realized. It was too dark to read them but from the faint outline of the pictures he could tell they were from films he knew. It was so cold he began to shiver and she came over to him, wrapping her arms around him. She had taken off her top and was naked this time. He brought his hands up her back, feeling each link in her spine through the skin. There was no fat on her body.

"Man, it cold."

"Well get in the bed then."

The girl was frank, he had to give her that. He quickly undressed apart from his boxers and dropped into the bed, pulling the covers over him. She got in next to him and rested her head on his chest. Beginning to caress him there, she gradually moved her hand lower, down to his stomach and then to his legs, feeling Ben's response to her touch.

"You want me now then? Just stay real quiet." She slowly twisted in the bed and moved down his side, dropping her head towards his waist.

Ben smiled at the sweet prospect of her kiss. "Anything you say girl."

Eleven

Ash pushed the accelerator down, making the engine scream. They were joining the motorway but he shot out of the filter road and straight to the fast lane. Horns sounded behind them but the car picked up speed and he left the traffic he had stalled far behind. The grey field of three-lane motorway stretched ahead of them and Curtis glanced at the speedometer as the needle curved into high figures.

"You rush a bit don't you?"

"Well t'was you that kept me waitin'. We have to be there noon." Ash looked nervy. He had been leaning on the front door of the flat when Curtis showed, fresh from breakfast with Amanda and had insisted they left he at once. Curtis had climbed into the passenger side of the car and noticed the two bags on the rear seat.

"You have a change of clothes in there then 'cause I been in these all night, sah?"

It was a joke, but there was no smile from Ash. Instead he'd gunned the car into action.

"Shit man, I just remember my phone. I leave it in the hurry."

"Yeah, well you no need it where we going."

Curtis would have insisted they return, but Ash looked hassled and he was right anyway. Calls would only be a distraction.

When they were out of town a few miles and the traffic had thinned down to the odd truck in the slow lane, he motioned to the bags in the back.

"You better deal with that right now."

Curtis reached back and pulled one of them into the front. It was a heavy sports bag with a steel zipper. He peeled it back and pushed the sides wide open.

The bag was stuffed with thick wads of money. Each flat pad was an inch thick and he caught the glow of green fifties. Curtis kept cool but the sight of the money made his heart pound and he let out a low sigh. He started working it out. Each pack must have one hundred fifties at least and there were hundreds of packs. He didn't need to go through his maths to know there was plenty of money between his legs.

Ash turned from the wheel and saw the open bag. "A ras. The other bag man."

He was still on edge, Curtis almost expected him to try and clip him for seeing the cash.

"Well, how me know? You just said get the bag."

"Just zip it up and toss it back. Bring the other now."

He did as instructed and placed the bag carefully on the rear seat. When they had met in the park, money had been discussed but nothing like this. This changed the situation somewhat. Suddenly the dream of the high game had turned to reality and Curtis realised just how much money was at stake. Carl must trust him implicitly.

The other bag was heavier and he had to bring both arms around to lift it into the front. Even when he had done so, he stared back at the other bag, in awe of it. Soon, he thought to himself, money like that would be nothing. The thought excited him. The new bag was of the same design and he rested it on the floor between his knees before opening it. He saw steel. The shiny barrel of a revolver and a stained wooden handle were resting in the bottom of the bag. For a few seconds he studied it. There was only one gun and two yellowing, cardboard boxes which he assumed held the cartridges. The sight was the equation to him. There was the money in the back, here the means of securing it. Balance returned, as the money on its own was just too good to be true.

"Well, there you go, boy. Now you one of the real bad man." Ash was sneering. He had lit a fat joint, pulled from his shirt pocket and his head was swathed in smoke. The skin of his face looked dry and leathery now that Curtis could study him up close. He wore a round leather hat, old style and the collar of his jacket was turned up, so only part of the face was visible but Curtis could see the wide grin.

"Ain't no big thing."

"Yeah, well, you never use one."

"Where yours, or you not carry?"

It was almost an insult and Ash paused for a second. Both of them listened to the whistle of the engine and the crackle of the seeds burning as Ash inhaled. It was straight bush. He passed it to Curtis.

"Maybe I do ride you a bit, C. I carry mine already." He patted his jacket, disclosing the rough shape of a gun. The tension had eased and Ash broke into talk about the meet. He knew Curtis was due a beating anyway. That would cut him down a bit, but Ash didn't think too harshly of him as it was. He had the courage to answer back and he was going into this deal blind. That meant he had something about him as far as Ash could see.

"Should be no need of it anyway, I feel. We only swapping the bags, but money a Carl and it everything he have, so you watch over it, yeah? When we a reach I do all the talking, maybe go off for a while, so you just sit with the money an' take it slow."

"I can do that, you no a fear."

The car darted back across the lanes to take a slip road. Ash was still doing well over a hundred and the thinner road made it feel even faster, as the trees flew past only yards from his window. The country was a dull brown. To Curtis it looked as though the soul had been torn out of it by industry. He could see the scars in the earth from mining as the fields rolled off to the horizon. This was not his world. In a few hours the bubble of the car would carry him back to town in luxury and he turned his eyes away from the grim vista, thinking of money, Amanda and the gun he already had with him, safe inside his leather jacket. He smiled at the thought of drawing it now, waving it under the driver's nose and shouting at him. *Me carry already you kwashi*!

But Curtis knew how little secrets could prove to be valuable and said nothing, just pulled on the joint. Ash rolled strong and he felt the surge through his blood as the bush whispered around his body. Reaching down to the bag he removed the gun and wedged it into his other inside pocket. Now he was packing two and the image of a bandit with double holsters made him smile.

They came down to a roundabout and Ash took the exit for the centre of town. Though the scenery was devoid of colour, there was a piercing winter sun shining down, setting out the lines of the trees and the odd building they passed. The bush he had smoked gave the light an even greater intensity and Curtis had to cover his eyes with his forearm.

Ash slowed and took a left. They rumbled along a thin lane with hedgerows on either side, splashing through large puddles.

"This the country, for sure."

"No peekin' eyes to see what a go on my friend."

Ash took a right and the road thinned into a muddy lane. Now they were rolling past a low stone wall with a hedge running along the top. They came to a break in it and Ash pulled into a driveway. On either side was a stone pillar, each with a weather-beaten statuette on top. Curtis could just make out the shape of a pyramid before they pulled into the yard.

The car stopped opposite a large farmhouse that surrounded them on three sides. A tall barn door made up the quartet of walls.

As soon as they pulled in Curtis saw three men approach and come up to the glass. One man opened his door and stood back to let him out. He was tall, wearing a long leather coat and heavy boots. One arm was under the coat, a shotgun perhaps. He was young with a fresh face and dredds.

"You reach then."

They were led into a large kitchen, the man who had spoken in the lead and the two others following the newcomers. At first sight they had all looked similar, dressed for the country, but as they entered the house they pulled off their coats and displayed the bright colours he was more used to. They were all young. Ash was definitely the oldest there, but they carried themselves tall, pulled-up and proud. Curtis carried the money bag. He thought they might sit at a table that dominated the centre of the room to do the swap but the lead man beckoned to him once he had dumped his coat on a chair. He carried a long barrelled rifle, gripped to his side, military style. Curtis stared at it, trying to look like it was no big thing that the man had it. This was a new game for him, but he set his face and stared him out. He was going to have to learn to treat this as natural and part of the code was never to look impressed. He wouldn't have blinked if the guy had stuck a machine-gun in his face.

"You like the farmhouse bit then?"

He waved his arm around the room and Curtis scanned it. There was a large fireplace, the table, a stove and some shelves with packets and jars lining them. The floor was a rough stone and the place looked period throughout. He had seen pictures of rooms like this in magazines where people wanted to go back to an old traditional way of living. It seemed dumb to him, going back to the past.

"It just a front, boy. Come now." He walked off to a corner of the room that was hidden in darkness. The ceiling was low like a cottage so there was not much light. As he approached the wall a dark square slid back about six foot high and he stepped through.

Curtis followed nervously. An exit would be hard to make in this place.

They walked down a thin corridor of stone with bare bulbs set in the roof giving what little light there was. It was low and they had to stoop, but after a few turns they came to a corner and went through into another room. Curtis had to step down two steps and then looked about him. It was like a club. There were five or six men lounging on sofas or by a thin bar at the far end of the room, at least thirty feet away. It seemed to be circular but the lighting was very soft and he found it hard to see everything as there were slatted partition walls between each group of seats. He could see enough to know it was lavish though. There was a thick carpet and the furnishing was of the kind you would find in a hotel lobby in town with plants and glass tables. The thing that amazed him more than the location of this idyll in the bowels of the farmhouse was the noise.

Music was pumping from a system to his left almost at club volume and even though it was only around noon there were two girls on a small, wooden dance-floor. They were showing, being watched by the guys slumped in chairs. The conversation was loud, and even though Curtis had a gun stuck under each arm and a bath-tub of money stuffed in the sports bag he felt rather insignificant.

For a few seconds he and Ash just stood there taking it in, and then a man a few yards off sitting in a sofa, pulled himself up and strolled over. Their escort dropped back, as though they were not allowed to enter and Curtis noticed they were the only ones displaying weapons in the crowd.

"You boys want a drink, maybe? Man should always have a wet throat when him talk business." He led them over to the bar, both of them staring round at the scene. "You town boys think you know the deal but we better off here man. A real nice thing I have here. Me called Red, cause of me temper, man."

He had motioned them onto some stools and it was a bit quieter here. Dressed in a blue suit, Curtis had at first thought the man might be tame but once he spoke he had to change his mind. It was a thick rasping voice, as though he had problems breathing, but this gave it menace. His face was fleshy and he was balding on top, probably in his forties. As he finished speaking he broke into a hearty laugh and slapped Ash on the back. Curtis was glad to be on the next seat. Ash looked winded. The man caught the look in his eyes.

"You still a pickney, boy. Don't try to look behind my eye there." It seemed he might leap on him, so crazed he looked but the next second he was calm and his voice dropped to a quiet bass. "What you drink then?"

"White rum."

Ash looked round at him.

"Well, me no a drive."

Red laughed at the remark then slipped to the end of the bar and reached over for a bottle. He came back and stood next to Curtis, towering over him in the lumpy suit. A huge fist circled the bottle as he lowered it gently to the bar. Curtis turned his neck to face the man and was staring at his chest. As he looked up to the eyes he saw a purple ridge of tissue on Red's neck. A network of thick scars wound up from under the tight collar of his shirt. Curtis swallowed hard.

"Oh, you see the scar then? That a message for you there, you see? Man try to cut my throat you hear, few years back. Him sneak up on me asleep and cut me. Him good with the knife but him never finish the job. I bury him in me back garden, you hear? Drink your drink, boy. Me have a little talk with your man for a minute."

Ash stood up and followed the broad back of the man off to the side of the room and through a thin door. Once they were out of sight he nudged the sports bag at his feet further under his stool and looked around him.

The busy atmosphere of the room had changed. The presence of Red had taken up his concentration and in the meantime nearly all the relaxed inhabitants of the room had left. The three men from their arrival were on a sofa by the entrance, staring across at him, crammed together on the soft leather. The middle man rested a rifle between his legs, pointing at the ceiling. Curtis felt a mounting tension and turned back to the bar, not knowing how to react to the change in the mood or whether it was significant or not, but his movement was interrupted by a sharp pain just beneath his shoulder. He tensed his muscles to turn but the pain grew worse, like someone pushing a hard object into his back. He didn't need to guess what it was. The gun would blow a hole in him if he moved and Curtis felt vulnerable, like a man with no will.

"Easy, boy. You just the carry man, no hero."

It was Red's voice, but where had he come from and what had happened to Ash? There must have been another route round the back of the bar that he had missed. He cursed himself for not checking the other doors or keeping his bearings in the place. The one time when it would have helped.

Now he heard Red's low tone so close he could feel the breath on the back of his neck and his body set like stone.

"You have a gun, I think."

Through the corner of his eye he could see the trio on the sofa, staring at him, motionless. There was no one else in the room now and he felt almost embarrassed as Red fingered his jacket and slipped the gun Ash had brought in the car for him out of the pocket.

It was too easy. He even knew that there was just the one and which side it was on, must have been told, as he didn't check under Curtis's right arm where the other gun was hidden. Now it made sense. The sudden rush of awareness gave him a new energy. For a second he had faltered. Red had scared him earlier, with the scars on his throat and the bass growl in his ear, but now he knew it was a cross he felt angry. Red was no big man, just another gangster trying to rip him. Ash was dropping him for dead meat, the guy who would put up no resistance once the gun was taken. A guy with no face.

There was no hesitation. Like a directive instinct he knew he must fight. Even though he was out of his normal patch and the odds were leaden against him, this was his creed. No man could be allowed to scare him, no matter what the situation.

"You mess wid a bad man, you get MASH!"

He threw himself off the stool, tearing at the gun hidden under his arm and turning on Red who stood gaping, startled to see the flash of metal. Curtis was fast. The three on the sofa came to life and started to rise to their feet, twenty yards across the room. Red brought the metal barrel in his fist up to his chest but by then Curtis had swept the butt of his revolver into the side of Red's nose, cracking the bone like chalk. Red lifted fat hands to his face, bellowing but still standing. He had enormous strength to withstand the pain and remain on his feet and Curtis knew he hadn't yet put him out of the game. As the blood seeped through Red's linked fingers, trying to hold his nose in one piece, Curtis drew the gun back and struck him again with the trigger guard, this time on the forehead above the eye. He had to lean forward on his toes to reach the big man's brow. This time blood spilled down his face like a burst dam, filling the eye socket with a thick stream. Red fell to the floor, broken, blood making a wide delta on the carpet.

Though the two blows had taken only a second to commit, the three armed men were half-way across the room, one of them stooping and pulling the rifle to his shoulder to take aim.

Curtis turned to face them. There would be no chase. In the space of the room he guessed his weapon was far superior to a rifle and he pushed himself back onto the bar, lifted his arm and without sighting any one of the three only yards from him, pumped the trigger.

At first, all he knew was the noise.

This was not the pop of a TV detective gun battle. The gun was a thunder in his head like a blow and he could hear nothing after the first shot. The handle bucked savagely, straining at his wrist and the flash from the muzzle lit up the room. He fired three shots. There was no way he could miss, the three were in a block, at point-blank range almost. They could see the flash of the gun light up his face, giving his contorted features the look of one possessed by shadows.

The front man had been hurtling towards him but ran into the volley as though it were a brick wall. It caught him straight, just beneath the ribcage, in the centre of his abdomen. All Curtis saw was the ruffle of his shirt, then a jet of blood and tissue flew out from his back and the man was picked up feet from the ground. The other bullets padded into him before he landed, a crumpled mess. Directly behind him the next man tried to change his course by throwing himself to the side but stumbled over the fallen man. He pulled himself from the floor and ran back for the door. Curtis was still rigid, ready to fire but did nothing as the man escaped. The last man had been preparing to shoot but dropped his gun and tried to turn. He had never seen a man shot before and his will to fight had collapsed at the sight of the carnage.

Curtis stepped forward and brought the gun up so his arm was straight out in front of him. He aimed at the back of the man's head as he retreated but again did not fire. The shot was clear but Curtis had no need to kill—the room was clear now. Despite the flood of energy from the fight he had managed to keep calm. He looked around him. Two of them were out on the ground, the dead man near his feet. Curtis had never seen death before but it was unmistakable. No man could lie that way. Red was finished for the moment, he didn't have much of a face left but the adrenalin rush steeled Curtis against the sight. He stood still, silent, surveying the damage. Smoke from the blasts curled around the shivering figures on the floor and he took in the image. He wanted to remember it, for it to be engraved on his memory. This was his first, victorious battle and the buzz of the action washed over his body. He had known he would not fail, this was a true test and he had come through.

The sound of steps running down the stone corridor broke the calm. He picked up the sports bag and ran to the office door where Ash and Red had gone before.

It was a small room with a desk and two chairs on either side. Ash had gone. A thin door was half open on the other side of the room and he made for it, desperately trying to gain his sense of direction so he could find a way out. He pulled it shut behind him and looked for a lock but there was only bare wood. His pursuers would not be delayed. Breathing hard he examined the hallway he was in. It was dimly lit by a weak bulb and the walls were rough brick, he could touch both walls by putting his arms out it was so thin. This was not a good place to be trapped and his heart began to race. He had just shot a man, was carrying a cheap sports bag which contained tens of thousands of pounds and had been betrayed by his team. Men with guns were probably crashing into the room just behind him and his legs were starting to feel like soft dough. The strength was beginning to fade from his body and he glanced at the gun in his fist, his mind racing. Time now to take the pressure, to earn the reward he dreamed of—but a chill was seizing him, the cold touch of violence.

He rushed down the hall and round a corner, running headlong into a heavy, steel door. It was open a crack and he inched round it, tugging the bag behind him. Voices echoed down the hall from the office and with a frantic push he closed the door and dropped the bolt. For a time he was safe as they would have to go around the obstacle. Even a bullet wouldn't pass through the metal. As his head sank to breathe in air his body tensed and he spun round, the gun raised automatically. He had heard a scraping sound behind him.

Ash was on the floor, lying in the dirt, blocking the hall. His big frame was bent in pain as he clutched his stomach. Curtis looked down the passage beyond him. He could see a crack of light about twenty yards away—daylight. The thought of escape filled his mind like a swimmer desperate for air, pulled down by the tide. He wanted out of this rat tunnel with its musty scent and broken brick. First though, he had to deal with Ash.

His hat was missing and a bald dome showed his age. He was a dying, old man, clutching his belly, with his eyes rolled back in pain. Violent gasps of air rushed across his lips.

"Curtis, get me to the car, boy. Man deal me a cut."

His voice was weak, a plea. Curtis looked to the floor and saw a black river trailing across the pitted concrete, already running round his shoes. Ash was bleeding to death.

"You set me up ya fuck." Even though he felt hatred this was mingled with pity. His face was that of a young boy finding a wounded animal.

"We both been set up a now. Zack stick me like a ras fool. You only s'pose to get lick a few times then me say we set up, Carl a fuck wid all the money gone an' me step in. The white man him fuck us both C., an' Red stick me like a pig. Look at me man! Big hole in ma belly!" His words were slow and raspy, punctuated by low sobs.

"You done Ash but me still can get out."

He couldn't help him. Lifting his foot he shoved him in the ribs, turning him over, then reached into the man's trouser pocket for the keys. They felt wet. A quick glance showed they were coated in blood. Curtis wiped them on the man's shirt collar.

"Me dig up."

He stepped over him and staggered to the end of the hall. Ash was so weak now he couldn't bring his voice up to more than a whisper as he looked at the young man's back fading in the dark.

"Me see you down the road boy, down the road."

He was out in the courtyard, the sunlight burning his eyes after the dark of the passage. From a few wooden steps at the end of the hall he had reached a wide grill and crawled out, finding himself in the corner of the yard. The strain of the battle and chase were telling and he had to lie in a heap for a few seconds trying to muster some strength. Ash was forgotten, a dead weight, a dying traitor.

"See him dere?"

The two men from the interior were by the door they had first entered on their arrival, only yards away from him. They burst into action, fresh for the fight. Somehow they had found courage after running from the last encounter. He could see the excitement in their faces as they lifted the dull black shapes of guns and braced their legs on flagstones by the door.

He stared at them, motionless. The car was still parked where Ash had left it, gleaming in the hard sunlight, but he couldn't bring himself to move. Should he fight? Was there a chance? The questions ran through his head and he saw Red's nose shatter, spots of blood striking his own cheek, like running back a film in his head. He knew each second of thought was costing him the chance for life but still couldn't bring his legs to move. Then his choice was made for him and he understood why his attackers were feeling brave.

With a wild bark the courtyard exploded. The men opposite each had a yellow blur planted at their waist, screaming like a chainsaw. The wall behind him shattered. Dust and chippings flew from the brick, glass broke and the ring of the bullets bouncing off the floor made him lift his hands to block out the sound. They had machine guns. In the flood of noise, amidst the chaos, he had a sudden, clinical wave of thought and threw himself to the car door and clambered inside. The guns let loose a swarm on the car. The windscreen shattered and he felt the impact of lead, ripping into the seats, smashing the front lights and puncturing the door frame. He buried his head by the wheel and rammed the key in, feeling a thousand, tiny shards of glass raining on his head and shoulders. The engine broke into life. He could only just hear the roar of revs over the rhythmic pulse of the guns. Ramming it into first he lifted the clutch and floored the accelerator, looking over the wheel by just an inch or two. There was a rush of wind as the car picked up speed, even in the tiny space of the yard. He pointed the nose of the car at the fire of the guns.

The yellow flash from the muzzles stopped and he caught the look of horror on their faces as he flew towards them but they had no choice but to dive out of the way. The front end of the car mounted the porch and rolled closer, smashing into the farmhouse wall. Either side of the bonnet the men dragged themselves to their feet, stunned by his daring and looked around for the discarded weapons, but now he was reversing. They dived onto the front of the car in some mad attempt to stop him. He rolled back off the steps, pumping the accelerator to the floor. Curtis was blind to their movements. He had only escape on mind as he heard another gun open up on the car. There was a man firing from a first floor window, leaning out to try and pick aim. Curtis could see him through the shattered glass of the windscreen as he scraped out of reverse and back to first, scrabbling with the wheel to steer for the narrow opening of the driveway. There was too much going on for him to deal with. The courtyard was a carnival of gunfire, screams of anger and howling engine. Without pausing he skidded off to the opening, steering with his left arm and lifting his revolver over the ledge of the door, knocking out a block of fractured glass as he took rough aim on the man at the window. He pulled the trigger, not counting the shots or really looking where they went, but the blind shooting distracted the sniper's fire.

He was almost free.

As he turned, the men on the bonnet fell away and were sent spinning into a corner. He pushed his foot hard against the floor and felt the breeze rush onto his face, hurtling down the lane away from the farmhouse. Only then did he shake the bag from his arm and settle in the seat. He lifted a hand to his brow and pushed it back through his hair then reached for the rear-view mirror to study his face. It had a thick crack running through the middle but he saw the shape of his head and flash of his eyes in a clear segment. However, he did not linger on the view. Something had distracted him. The left hand holding the mirror for his curious eyes looked disfigured and unreal. It was twisted, dirty. He pulled it back in front of his face and studied it.

His first finger was gone, down to the bottom knuckle, leaving a stub of bone in the socket. He felt no pain. He just stared at it, looking up now and again to make sure the car was rushing him along the road.

Twelve

Ben stared in through the bakery window for a long, hungry moment then examined the change in his palm. He had less than he needed. He started walking for home, down the highstreet and towards the mess of streets that snaked to his own. His father would be around, probably watching afternoon sport on the television and this always made him talkative. After watching his team get beaten he would be in a brooding state, just the time for a lecture on his wayward son. If, by some trick of fate, they were to win then the feeling of pride would produce the same lecture, his confidence would spill out in a speech.

The feeling of hunger and wish to delay his homecoming prompted Ben to change route, doubling back on the highstreet. He decided to check Mike. Maybe he could be persuaded to buy some food and front him the taxi fare. It was a grey, wintry afternoon and the wind was up, cutting through his light club-wear. He cursed himself for not wearing something more hardy.

Mike had finished work and was on his way out of the shop, setting the alarm when Ben called out to him. The record store was set off the main road, down a little alleyway and the wind roared between the walls, wrapping sheets of loose newspaper and trash around his legs as he fumbled with the key.

"I just catch you then. Where were you? Couldn't really hang around cause the girl wanted to go out to a club but I left a note for you."

Mike was still fiddling with the lock but nodded a hello.

"C'mon, man. It windy, you know."

"Yeah, yeah. I've been working all day, I'm beat."

"So you in just the right mood for some hot food."

"You what?"

The centre was packed and they had to wait a few minutes for a table, Mike muttering about the expense. It was now late afternoon and the neighbourhood youth was showing out. The age range was spread between the kids still at school to those who had just left or been out a year or two. It was almost a reunion at times but Ben and Mike were entering the stage of finding it all a bit juvenile. Ben liked it more but only because he could flirt with the girls who sat around spending hours sipping on a soft drink.

"Maybe that girl I deal with at the party here, Mikey."

"Nah, I don't see her or her friends."

Mike was looking on edge. He had borrowed from Adam which was always foolish and then stayed at Bliss till closing time, getting drunk. The day in the shop had stretched on forever and what he had earned would be just enough to cover the debt. Now Ben was borrowing and that could take months to reappear. Ben was not the most reliable debtor. The casual way Ben had spent the entire profit from the sale the day before was annoying as well. After all, Mike had set it up and received nothing.

Their food arrived and Ben launched into it with a fierce energy. Both of them were hungry and said nothing whilst they ate but as soon as Ben had finished chomping, he began to tell Mike of the Celia exploits. The tale of conquest made Mike irritable. As though the loan and the stand-up at the bar were not enough, it was he who had invited Celia to the meet and now had to listen to the tale of how Ben enjoyed fleshy contact with her in graphic and minute detail. To make things worse, he had enjoyed a particularly romantic fantasy that morning, with Celia the main recipient of his ardour in a shady forest clearing.

He stared through the glass that separated the restaurant from the domed concourse, watching the girls float past in their little groups, pretending not to take too much interest in Ben's tale.

"Man, when I take her from behind, man, I lift up this bra or thing she wear round her titty anyway . . ."

"Ben, man, for fuck's sake . . ."

"No, serious. Me pick this top up and string it through her teeth then ride her round the room like a donkey, man."

He was being deliberately coarse, knowing it wound Mike up. His friend's distant look was a giveaway that he was thinking of the pleasures that eluded him.

"She was game for it, Mikey, nothin' put her off."

"Yeah, I heard enough now Ben. Just keep it to yourself will you."

Ben reflected on his time with the girl. Perhaps he had been a bit base for Mike's benefit. She didn't deserve it. His story was inflated in some respects. After they had jumped into bed she had given him a quick climax with her mouth, very adeptly, and then fallen asleep in his arms. There was a chance that she was just anxious to calm him down and had chosen the quickest way to do so, knowing he would be restless otherwise. Ben had a suspicion that this was the case but couldn't be sure. All he knew was that he wanted to experience the rest of her body.

He had slept soundly and was woken by her dressing in the dim morning light. With his eyes open just enough to see her, he watched as she delicately tended to her dressing, then as she came over to wake him he jumped up and wrestled her to the bed, making her squeal with laughter at the surprise. She had left for work and let him sleep on, letting himself out hours later and her trust impressed him. Who was to say he wouldn't search through her things? Ben had liked her gesture. Celia was appealing to him as a long-term prospect, though he didn't consider telling her this for one instant. Partly for his own pride but also because he couldn't really tell how she felt about him.

They had arranged to meet in a few days time for a meal and the task of assembling enough money to pay for it was already troubling him. Mike was no rich-kid at the moment that was for sure and increasing his credit-worthiness with him was impossible. Mike knew what state his finances were in. Maybe Curtis could front him something but he still owed him for the hash. The thought of another mugging did not appeal either. He had howled with laughter when Mike told him his story but there was a side to it Ben didn't like. Turning the problem over in his mind he stared absently through the glass into the packed concourse.

Through the crowd of people he caught a glimpse of a man. There was something familiar about him. Ben tried to recall the face, hidden by hair and a thick beard. Who did he know with a beard? There was only one possibility. This could be his financial salvation. It was the Sheltham freak, Paul.

"Mike, dig up man, come now."

"Hey, what's the deal?"

"Settle up, me be outside making a dollar."

He ran round the table and pushed his way out of the door. For a second he had lost the head with its wild mane of knotted hair but soon saw it reappear, going into the walkway to the shopping centre. He charged over, breaking through the crowd and tapping the hippy on his shoulder.

"Paul my man, good to see you. I think you just made my day."

Paul looked as though his brain took a moment to register the presence of Ben by his side, then a warm smile spread across his face. Ben became aware of a strong odour coming from Paul's trainers like his feet were in a state of decay but gritted his teeth. He needed the money.

"Oh. Yes I do remember you, don't I? You struck me I think, a few days ago, wasn't it?"

Paul still sounded like an RAF boy even in the midst of a leisure centre, dressed in a raggedy navy sweater and filthy jeans. Ben stared deep into his eyes, trying to reach the part of the brain still active.

"Listen up. I didn't just hit you did I . . ."

"Oh you mean Astrid. She's left me again."

Paul looked a bit upset.

"Astrid, no, no I mean some smoke I had you know. And all that trouble you put me through. I think you should take a quarter off me."

The hippy looked frightened. He shone wide eyes around him, fearful of talking about a drug in public. He felt nervous away from his domain in Sheltham. Ben saw his worry and was disgusted. This was typical of the white smoker.

"I talk about draw where I please, boy. So you want some, yeah?"

"Well maybe. I do have a little money."

"Excellent."

Mike had arrived next to Ben and was leaning over

Paul with a glint in his eye. He had picked up on the atmosphere and joined Ben in presenting a determined sale.

"My colleague here will wait with you in a bar we know whilst I fetch the draw. How does that sound?"

"Well perhaps . . ."

"That'll be forty up front then."

Paul was intimidated by the two but had been thinking of a smoke anyway so he started to rummage in his pocket. "I'll give you twenty up front as you see wise to do so and the rest when you come to the bar. Wouldn't mind a drink either." He handed over a bruised note and Ben smiled.

"Mikey, Bliss, twenty minutes."

The hand was hurting now. A wave of pain shuddered along his arm every few seconds, rushing to his chest and head, making his whole body tense up. The only bandage available was his own clothing and he had torn a long strip from his shirt, wrapping it around the stump and finally securing it at his wrist. He had never felt pain like this. The finger must have been lost as he ran to the car but in his flight he had not noticed the hit.

On top of the dull tension of pain he felt weak and guessed the blood loss may be affecting him. It was a few hours since the fight now. Yet after all this, the agony of the cotton rubbing the remaining tissue and cartilage, the blood thinning in his veins, the dull ache of fatigue and stress throughout his body and the realization that he was maimed for the rest of his life, there was something far more distressing. What could he do now? He had sobered from the adrenalin frenzy and was thinking clearly. His situation was desperate. If the police still hadn't been involved then that meant the gang were intending to take care of him themselves and he had hurt them badly. Carl was not a patient man and Curtis could see the difficulty in explaining how this had happened when Ash had been stabbed and was not around to talk. There may be no time for story telling. He had the money but needed to rest and to eat something. It would be dark soon and the car was useless. It was known, it had no lights, the windscreen was gone and it looked like something from a gangster movie. It was peppered with holes. He sighed and dropped his head down to his lap.

After the escape he had made for the motorway but had soon changed his mind. Above twenty miles an hour the car let in a gale of icy, country air which felt like sand in his eyes. He had no flying goggles and that was the only way to drive something with no glass. Then there were other considerations. In a movie, Curtis would have blasted his way out and then the next scene would be him reclining on a bed being fed grapes by a blonde in a sequined dress. Fact was he was at least eighty miles from town and running scared. He also had a shattered hand and was wise enough to know that if he didn't fix it right away he was in big trouble. Curtis had come from a hard path and he had known other fighters. He had seen people injured and not tend to their wounds and knew about blood infection and how fast you could lose a limb. A strip from his shirt was not going to do.

He couldn't decide about the gun. Dumping it would be wise right now but it may be a mistake if the situation was to change and that could happen at any instant. At the moment he was parked in a field, just off the road before a small group of houses and he had visions of a car screaming round the corner any second and someone trying to put a bullet in his brain. They must be checking the roads for him. He had cruised for a while, getting rapidly lost and was trying to think in as clear a way as he could manage. He needed help.

To his right was a pay phone. The sight of it had drawn him like a magnet as he had driven by and he had been sitting here, thinking of his options for the last twenty minutes. He was out on his own and knew now that all this was the real test of the bad man. Pulling the trigger had been easy. It would be a long night trying to stay alive.

Ben shut the door lightly, sliding the latch into place with practised stealth. He could hear the drone of the sports results from along the hall and was glad that it would cover the light step of his shoes on the stairs. A change of clothes was essential. A thick, grainy sensation had come over him from the late night and he longed for the feel of soft, clean cotton on his skin.

"Ben, boy. That you, then?"

There was a shuffle and his father appeared at the foot of the stairs. He wore his slippers and a brown cardigan, making him look like a pensioner.

"Yes, it me. I busy though."

"Oh, you too busy to hear a message, then?"

He looked back over his shoulder, rushing up the stairs to escape the obligatory lecture and was almost at the top when his father spoke.

"Who dat, then?"

"It Curtis, sayin' he need your help with something. Something downright unlawful, I suppose, is it?"

"I dunno what you mean."

He had come down the stairs to the small table where the phone rested. His father was at his side.

"Where the number, then?"

"No number, he call back in one hour."

That was typical. He was supposed to hang around for an hour waiting for the call and when it came it would probably be another session out East or something similar. Curtis never rang to be sociable these days.

"Well, you tell him I had to go out, people to see."

His father looked angry. A black hue came over his face and his frame started to shake. Ben knew this look. It was the post-sport lecture for sure.

"No, you stand there and listen."

He was making a break for his room.

"You stand there and listen, or I change the ras locks when you go out. Now you come in, it almost the night and you been out since yesterday. Not only do you treat me like I is some kind a message service and this place a hotel, but Curtis the only real friend you have. That boy Mike is a fool and runs round after you like a child. Now Curtis sound like him need your help . . ."

"Curtis big man, you know . . ."

"Man sound like him need help."

"Well, if he calls, which is unlikely anyway, tell him I down Maxine's if it urgent. He can find me there."

"But Ben, we have to talk. Where you been for these last days? You been looking for work maybe, my ass. You just run round and go nowhere. You got to sit down and talk to me."

"Later. I be round tomorrow, we talk then."

"That no good. By the time you up I be out and . . ."

Ben's bedroom door closed at the top of the stairs.

The house was dark apart from a kitchen light at the back. Maybe someone was preparing a meal. His stomach felt like a dry, leather pouch it was so empty. It was set back from the other houses that made up the village, and the distance was enough to make it unlikely that any disturbance would be heard. He checked that there was a car in the driveway and was relieved to see an ancient hatchback, then walked through the front garden to a large porch and rang a bell button imbedded in the brick. Out here in the country the silence was acute and the volume of his breathing alarmed him. He must try to look as though he had been in an accident and not a gun battle. It all depended on what news had leaked out from the shooting, but if there had been any reports then only a blind man would fail to recognise him.

He heard steps padding along to the door and after a few twists of a lock he was bathed in the light from the hallway. A young girl looked at him with a blank expression.

"My car came off the road."

"Yeah, you look a mess." She did not look impressed and kept her hand on the edge of the door, as if she would slam it shut at any moment.

"So, can I come in?"

There was a pause, then she backed away from the door and started walking back down the hall. He stepped in and followed her, feeling like something the dog brought in.

The kitchen was bright. It was lavishly done out with a bunch of white machines along one wall, a row of small windows and a square table covered in documents of some kind. Even the walls were a bright morning yellow. There were signs of the family, a cork board covered in bits of paper and some crayon drawings stuck on the fridge door. He had to squint for a second as he stood in the middle of the room, shielding his eyes. She was bending at a cupboard underneath the sink and came out with a tin biscuit box which she put down on the table.

"I was doing some school work."

She still had no expression on her face which puzzled him. He was covered in blood stains, had torn clothes and a dirty sports bag hanging from his shoulder but she looked at him like he was the milkman. He guessed she was about his age and through the strain of his predicament Curtis still observed her long hair and slim figure. She was pretty. The thought almost made him smile as he imagined her with no clothes, trying to make love to her with his broken body. This was no time for romance.

"You want me to ring for a doctor, then? They

wouldn't be here for ages anyway. We're miles from town."

"You're relaxed aren't you? Stuck in the middle of nowhere with a strange black man wandering round your house."

"I thought you looked trustworthy. Not everyone out here is suspicious of strangers you know." She fussed at the table, moving her work and opening the tin. "Sit down and I'll dress it."

"No, I do that. You get me something to drink, brandy or something. And have you got any food?"

"I could make you a sandwich." She was obliging anyway, if a bit frosty.

Curtis slumped in a chair and pushed the collection of bottles and packets from the box into a wide circle on the table. Time was catching up on him. Ben was due the call. He found a wide bandage and some strong antiseptic then walked over to the sink and peeled the tattered rag from his hand.

It was a funny colour. The blood streaming out of it had left it waxen and numb like a lump of rubber. Moving any of the remaining fingers was impossible but he could make the thumb tremble. The bleeding had abated for now and there was a thick clot of congealed blood coating the torn stump. He was reminded of a tree torn out by the roots, leaving an ugly scar in the earth.

He fingered the bottle of liquid and loosened the lid. This was going to be a screamer he knew, but he steeled his hand and clenched. The pain rose up like a serpent as he poured roughly half the bottle's contents onto the wound. That was the easy part. Now he flushed the hand with cold water from the tap until the wound was clear of most of the hardened blood. When it was free of the excess clotting he pulled the hand back and coated it once more with a flood from the bottle, and this time the pain made him shudder like ice on his soul. He dropped away from the sink, his knees giving way with the pain, but an arm stopped him falling and pulled him back to the chair. The girl had watched the entire process from just behind him and after seating him, began to wrap the hand with the bandage he had selected. She didn't flinch at the sight of the injury. Curtis still felt shudders of agony but the pain was slipping back gradually. When she had finished dressing the wound she handed him a thick tumbler and he took a gulp from it. The spirit felt like sweet medicine.

"Girl, you hardy."

She smiled at him. "If my father was here he'd have thrown you back into the street. But I think we have a duty to help others. I'm not going to ask you any questions either, probably best I don't know."

So she had realised his accident may have been more than a car crash. He smiled at her. "Well, that duty you talk about might get stretched a bit tonight."

Then he saw the reason for her helping him. The mention of her father had brought a look of fire to her eyes and he guessed at her mood. Curtis had grown up alone in life and this had made him observant of the way families worked, the pressures that could mount between people thrown together by blood ties. He saw the anger in her, imagined the father. Out here in the country she would dream of escape from the dull oppression of her parents. Curtis represented the unknown to her, a mystique she had dreamt of as her father droned on with brutal, ignorant authority. Curtis thought of her frustrations, the monotony of an existence isolated from other cultures and the temptations of youth.

His strength was returning as the hand settled down. A fantasy gripped him. He could stay in the house for a few weeks being nursed by her, slowly seduce her and take her body as his. Then the image of Amanda formed in his mind. The reward of her sweet skin the night before he left. That all felt like another lifetime, lost in some valley of his memory. The calming thoughts washed over him as sleep approached, sneaking up on his aching frame with its clever deceit but he shook himself out of it in time, still in control. He had to get back to town now, deal with Carl and fix his hand before time ran out on him. He needed the car. At first he would have just taken it, there would have been little she could do to stop him, but the girl had been charitable. She was at the fridge now, preparing him some food and he watched her soft movements. He had no desire to cause her distress.

"You want to sell your car, then?"

Bliss had been open all day, this being the weekend. It sold coffee in the afternoons and there were still a few people sipping from mugs and reading papers. Mike and Paul made straight for the bar and each took a stool.

"He won't be long will he? I don't really like bars particularly."

Mike just shrugged and asked the barman for a beer. At least he could get some money off Ben when he had completed the sale. A night of drinking appealed. The vulgar account of Celia's sexual performance had upset him as Mike had secretly thought her come-on in the shop was for real and it had even crossed his mind that she would be the one to tutor him in the act. Now that dream lay shattered at his feet he was not in good spirits. Being stuck with Paul for the next half an hour was not a huge temptation either.

On the way over here Paul had made some pretty strange remarks and Mike suspected his mental facilities were somewhat frazzled.

"Yes and I'll have a large vodka on its own please. Don't worry, I'll get these."

Mike had made no move for his wallet anyway.

"On its own?"

"Yes, you have to be able to taste the fellow. Mixer just gets in the way, I find."

"But Vodka has no taste. It's tasteless innit?"

"You are quite mistaken there. It has a delicate, oily quality. The essence of alcohol."

Mike turned and sighed at the fruitcake. His voice made him sound drunk already with its wild upper-class lilt. He was taking deep sips from his glass.

"Yes, I could tell you a few stories about drinking, that's for sure. Back in the old days when I was in there."

"Spare me, please."

"As you wish."

They moved over to a booth and sat in silence. Mike had plenty to dwell on. He was pondering another mugging, this time he might get lucky. However, there was still no way he could think of getting any real amount of cash together and he tried to trace a route around the problem. The safest bet was Curtis. He would be a big man soon and could possibly lend him a decent amount, but Mike had found their last meeting difficult. His attempt at bravado had just made him look silly and Curtis had thought him a fool, surely. Nonetheless, this was the only option.

"A what, Mike. You off in dreamland." It was Ben, slightly breathless, leaning on the table.

"Well, you reach quick. We've only just sat down."

"Yeah, me hold a minicab."

Of course, now he had the advance from Paul, Mike remembered.

"So, here you go Paulie!" Ben slid a small lump wrapped tightly in cling-film across the table, in full view of the bar.

"Please, not so obvious with it. It is the same material I smoked previously?"

"The very same, Paul." Ben stuck his palm out but Paul made a rather comical attempt to hand the rest of the money under the table, all the time looking around suspiciously, shooting glances around the bar. Ben and Mike sniggered. Anyone who knew Bliss would pay no attention to large amounts being bought and sold across a table. It was common. Ben knew a place where you could order it from behind the bar and it would be handed over with your drink, but Paul was a country boy. To him, this was reckless. It was afternoon now, so Ben had no anxiety about clowning around. The regular dealers wouldn't be there until nightfall. "Skin up then, Paul."

The laughter broke out in force now. Paul looked like a frightened lamb.

"You don't mean that, do you? Pretty daring in a public place I would have thought."

"No, relax. I jus' kiddin'." Ben pushed himself away from the table and stood tall. He had changed and felt ready for a night down at Maxine's on the back of Paul's money. "Well, me dig up. Gotta check with C. on something."

"What? You going round his yard?"

"Yeah, it on the way from Celia. Thought I might pass by her place. Never know my luck, boy."

Mike needed some money for the lunch he had bought and a tip for fixing up the deal. He knew that if he didn't mention it then Ben wouldn't and in other situations he would have let it pass. This afternoon though, Mike was not feeling in the mood to be ignored.

"I come with you, Ben. We need a little chat an' all, don't we?"

Ben looked hassled. He knew what was wanted and some money for Mike meant a chunk out of the wad, small as it already was. He would have said something, but Mike was standing and stepping past Paul.

"Sure, you come part of the way then. Paul now, listen up. You need some more you bell Adam like before, right? Safe man."

They turned and marched for the door, bracing themselves to the wind as they stepped out. Paul was left looking around him, thinking if he could remember the way home and nervously fingering the lump of plasticine Ben had just sold him.

The motor let out a shrill whine of protest as he pushed it to eighty. It was a tired-out heap, but it only had to get him back to town so he was not concerned about nursing it. The lights above him flashed past, each yellow beam he passed representing a step further towards his destination. His body was a mass of pain. The hand felt cold now and this worried him more than the agony of earlier. But he still had some strength. Through the blur of fatigue and confusion he had a purpose and would see it through.

His first thoughts after the fight had been to call Ben and then Amanda, but Ben had failed to turn up at his house and he could not rely on Amanda to be supportive of his going to see Carl if she knew how desperate the situation was. Knowing she was out for the afternoon, he had left a message on her machine telling her to wait by the phone when she got in. If he got through at the club then he could rest up with her. She was his safety clause.

The girl had not minded him taking the car. He gave her a sheaf of notes from the bag without counting it, then promised to leave it somewhere it would be noticed so she would get it back the next day. He hoped she didn't report it stolen straight after his departure, but she gave him a funny sense of loyalty. It would be interesting to meet people like that under different circumstances, he reflected.

Tucked in his jacket was the gun, fully loaded. The cartridges in the other bag were of the same calibre and he had dropped a box in the money bag for added security. The gun was his stability now, his foundation. It would see him through the next few hours.

Thirteen

There was no way he could get out of paying him at least a ten-spot. Mike had set up the ounce and bought him lunch, but it still hurt. One round at Maxine's and a bite to eat would cost him thirty. Then again, he still had the hash and he chuckled at the thought of Paul returning to the dank retreat in Sheltham for a furtive smoke only to discover that plasticine had limited use in his pipe. The hippy was dumb to trust him after the last fiasco, especially as Astrid was no longer on the scene to tempt the dealer back. Ben thought back on her kiss.

"So, you gonna see me right?"

"Uh. Oh yeah, sweet Mike, here you go." He handed him a bruised tenner. They were cutting through the backstreets of the patch, over to where Curtis lived. Ben felt as though he should look in after not waiting for the message. There was always the chance that Curtis needed a favour for a quick hand-out. Money was becoming important again.

"Well, I catch you down at Maxine's later."

"You what? Thought you wanted to see C."

"Nah. Got a few things to attend to. Say hello for me though." He stuffed the money in his pocket and then stepped off the pavement.

Ben watched him cross the street and walk down to the next corner. Mike was acting strange these days that was for sure. His figure disappeared around the corner and Ben turned to walk on.

Curtis had the ground floor flat in a row of smart townhouses. He had a cheap rent deal on the place and Ben was envious. If his father saw the usual kind of room he would get on the dole, he might think twice about threatening to throw him out, but he thought the flat Curtis had was normal. It had a small front garden hemmed in by a low fence and the front of the house was neat and well structured. There were no loose roof tiles or lazy brickwork in this area. Mainly professionals lived here and the street was always lined with expensive cars. Ben strutted up the path to the porch.

He could see Curtis's room by peering through the

front window, the curtains were wide open. This was the first sign that Curtis would not be answering the door. The second was an intermittent green flash from the dark interior, the message-machine was busy with calls. He could see nothing else in the room as it was night now and there were no lights on in his flat or the hallway. The dark had come down with stealth. Ben was not in the mood for waiting, anyway Curtis could be gone all week for all he knew. The chances of catching Celia in were slim now. She was probably back from work and getting ready to go out, but Ben decided to walk over anyhow to see if he could persuade her to join him at the club. All his tramping around surely couldn't be a complete waste of time. She might even give him the gift of the rest of her body which had escaped him the night before. He lifted up from the window and walked down the path.

"Boy you move an' I break your legs."

The bulk of a man blocked the end of the path to the street. It was dark but he could still see power in the arms and chest and he hesitated at the threat. For a moment he thought of rushing him but then chose escape as the wiser option. Ben was not the same as Curtis in his beliefs. If he was sober he would try to avoid a fight if he thought it was none of his concern and had no problem with respect or face in these matters. This man was no part of his dealings. The house next along had only a low partition wall separating it from Curtis's and he hopped over it and raced down the path. Ben was fast when he wanted to be, but no amount of speed would have rescued him from the second man who lurked just by the gate, ready for such a move. He ran straight into him and was picked up off the ground by arms like a crane. This guy was a monster, a seven foot wall.

"You no hear him deafy. He say he gonna break your legs like a ras insect."

Ben was gripped to the man's chest as if in a steel hug. There was no way to breathe with the pressure on his lungs and he could hear himself make little sobs, trying to say something. His feet were two feet off the ground, swinging wildly to find a grip.

"Put him down Alsash. Him have to talk, sah."

He was lowered to the floor and took deep gasps on the cold, night air. The two men flanked him. He stared at them to see if the faces were known but they were strangers to him. They were both older than him, maybe in their mid-thirties. The first man had dredds and a thick gold chain round his neck. It was worth more than Ben had earned in his lifetime. The face was hard, thin boned and with wary eyes. Though he was well built and slightly taller than Ben, he too looked a midget beside Alsash. The giant had his arms crossed like a sultan's bodyguard. Both men wore suits. They were cut for style though, not business.

"You gonna tell me straight, boy. Where this fuck Curtis, then?"

Ben was still winded and couldn't quite believe the question.

"What you want with him?"

"That my deal, pickney. You no need a fill your head with ras question. Man have need a find him and soon, so talk up."

"I don't know where he is. You saw me come round looking for him myself. I thought he was here."

"It right, Bunny. I mean, he wouldn't be here if he knew . . ."

"Settle down man. Me know that. But he may know about later, sah."

"Honest, I haven't seen him for days."

The three stared at one another and knew the conversation was over. Out in the street Ben felt the quiet as Bunny stared at him, trying to work out if the youth knew anything.

"Come now, man. We dig up. This boy know less than we." He turned to go, the giant following behind, but then spun round and spat on the pavement just in front of Ben's feet. "When we find the boy, Alsash gonna do that wid him head."

He was depressed. The situation had deteriorated utterly. *Don't go to pieces Zack*

Muttering to himself he wandered the loft. In his right hand he carried a bottle of whisky which he was steadily consuming. Zack could drink a lot of whisky without getting drunk and this was exactly the sort of time when he had the urge.

The phone had rung two hours ago and Zack had expected a happy Red on the line. He should be happy with close to a quarter of a million in cash as payment for scratching two amateur gangsters. However, Red was not only far from happy, Red was not talking. He was having his face re-shaped after some youth had pistol-whipped him and it was his second in command on the phone. The money had gone, along with one of their men who was now in a shallow grave. They were angry. Pressure was now on Zack to deal with Curtis. They had decided to keep it personal and the police would not be informed of the death—they were passing it over to him. As the voice informed him of the developments and how he would be held responsible from now on, Zack imagined Carl sitting at a big desk being told the whole story by an heroic Curtis, the money piled in front of him. Carl would figure it out and there would be a delegation sent forth to slap some wrists. He knew Zack had dealt with Red in the past, that was probably why it had taken him so long to go for the bait.

Even Ash had vanished. Red had split his belly open, but the man had crawled off and not been found, and though he could not survive the wound there was the potential for a very dangerous phone call.

Zack pictured Curtis in his mind and began to salivate with hatred for him. How was he to know there would be another gun? The youth had thwarted a perfect plan. Ash was stupid enough to believe he would be boss of a new team and he should have brought the job off for Zack, his greed being motivation enough. The money gone, Carl would be finished and would blame the absent Ash for his ruin, then Zack would step in, Curtis would be punished for his assault and everything would be tidy. Now there were dead men and a missing money bag. Curtis had to be intercepted before he reached Carl.

It had only taken Zack a few seconds to see the correct action to take. He had called Bunny. He and his partner were the only hired hands he knew who would work in that part of town and were known for results. They were also expensive, but then again there was some big money at stake and he had no choice. Zack was also toying with a last ditch solution but he was anxious to avoid it, if at all possible. That really would be difficult a—call to Carl.

The evening was rushing on and every minute brought Curtis closer to town. He was out there somewhere trying to make it to Carl. Zack walked up to the cold window, sticking his nose almost to the glass. To the horizon's limit the town was full of tiny lights, twisting and moving in the black. *This time, you have got to screw up* Curtis. *My future may depend on it.*

Fourteen

There was a band playing tonight and a line of people filled the pavement, waiting to get in but Ben gave the doorman a sly look and squeezed past the knot of people in the entrance. He was known as a friend of Curtis and Curtis was a friend of Carl so he got in, no trouble. Besides, they liked Ben at the door. He usually had a joke or amusing anecdote to tell. That was not the case tonight. Ben was in a hurry.

His meeting with the two searchers had scared him and he shot up the stairs and scanned the top bar, then went out onto the glass-walled balcony. Curtis was not up here and the downstairs room was so busy that it was impossible to distinguish individuals. The club was rammed. There was a sea of people shuffling to the beat, warming up for the band. Maxine's was small for a live music venue and a big name draw could pack it wall to wall. All the local youth was here and in different circumstances he would have been out on the dance-floor, cruising from one group of people to the next, just enjoying the atmosphere.

He should have waited at his house for him to call. This was no trivial problem as only desperate men would want to be chasing Curtis. Ben had to find him. He charged down to the main room and started checking faces, nodding a quick hello to people he knew as he passed.

Within a couple of minutes he had checked the entire space and it was clear he had not yet arrived, if he was coming at all. Ben thought it best to wait upstairs for him, so returned to the balcony and found a chair which provided him with a view of the dance-floor and the top bar. If he came he would head for Carl first so Ben kept a watch for the boss man as well as his friend.

There was the chance that Curtis would head elsewhere, maybe to his girlfriend, but Ben did not know her number or where she lived. He would sit patiently, keeping watch and hoping Curtis would stumble into him before he stumbled into the arms of the giant.

Mike sat down on the side of his bed and stared up at his fantasy. She was everything he saw in his dreams.

Ignoring the floor, covered in fraying record sleeves and magazines and looking past the dull wallpaper, he could almost see the golden sand and expanse of sapphire water of his beach-scene wonderland. Celia smiled at him.

Mike had doubled back towards home when he left, thinking of relaxing for an hour or two and getting to the club late. He had to stretch the money out anyway, being down to a tenner. His route had taken him down the highstreet just as the last shops were closing and a sudden temptation had seized him. He would pass the boutique Celia worked in and say hello. All that was on his mind was to see her and have a quick word. He knew Ben would forget her in a day or two and it seemed wise to maintain some contact. Maybe he could move in when there had been an appropriate gap in her fling with Ben. Mike harboured some fondness for her and had been encouraged by her flirting the last time they had met. Celia was older and represented womanhood to him, along with the pleasure he had yet to experience.

The shop was empty like the last time he had visited it and she stood at the same place, behind the low counter. To him the shop was her boudoir.

"So what bring you round? You have another message for me?"

He broke into a blush and she guessed the reason for his calling.

"Just thought I'd come in, say hello, you know. We only work a bit apart."

"Yes, but you finish a while ago don't you? So something else bring you back."

"Well . . ."

"Like, maybe you want to buy me a drink after I had a hard day at work?" She was smiling and putting on a half-length jacket, making ready to leave.

"Yeah, sure." This was better than he had hoped for. They went out into the street after she had turned out the lights and set the alarm and he made steps towards Bliss. The thought of just talking to her over a drink thrilled him, as the times before it had been a quick greeting or word for Ben and he had never considered a proper conversation.

She called to him. "What wrong with this place?" She pointed at a liquor shop at the other end of the street.

His heart rate doubled.

"What we doing there then?"

"Well, don't you have a place we can go?"

There was no turning back now. He had sensed there was some interest the first time he had been to her shop and now she was suggesting they went drinking back at his house. There was only the one obstacle.

"I think Ben may object to you an . . ."

"Ben not my master you know, boy. A girl can play the field as well as the man these days." She was up close to him in the street, speaking softly, her body almost touching his. "You afraid of him?"

It was a taunt. She was offering him his fantasy. The wind curled around them in a sudden gust and he lifted up his arms and wrapped them round her waist.

"It's not far."

Then there was the rush home with both of them in an expectant silence. Every few steps he would steal a kiss from her lips and sweep his hand down to her thigh, whilst she pushed him away and told him to wait. It was going to happen for him at last and with the very girl from his dreams. He would ply her with some of the wine clutched under his arm then slowly undress her, savouring each new expanse of velvet skin as it was revealed.

His mother was in a back room of the house, reading a magazine and he muttered hello to her whilst Celia crept up the stairs to his room. His father was out. That was good as his mother would probably fall asleep for an hour or two and there would be no interruptions.

Now he sat looking at her from the bed, trying to control his breathing. Her face was full of humour at the scene, sneaking past his mother and hiding in the room. It was similar to the routine at her own home and she did not expect this of a guy. His boyish expression of anticipation made her curious. He was looking at her as though she was a statuette and she stepped up to him, putting a finger across his lips.

"If you a virgin then just nod your head."

The answer made her let out a giggle.

"Well I make it something you remember then."

His room was out of his perception, he could only see the girl. She stood, legs wide apart and began to remove her clothes. It took only seconds then she was naked. There was no shame on her face, Celia had decided she would have sex when and with whom she pleased, without worry. And she was proud of her body. Though she was now in her early twenties she still had the tight lines of a teenager and her breasts were firm. He stared at the mirage. Any anxiety about loyalty to

Ben had evaporated long before they reached the house and now she was naked, he felt his desire surge up like a mushroom cloud. His life had meant nothing up until this point. Celia was about to take him to a higher plateau of pleasure than he had ever known and as she took a light step towards him his body began to tremble with energy.

"Mike! You better get down and see to the door, right now! Curtis wants to have a word."

Seeing the winding streets of his patch once more cleared his head and brought a little strength back to his body. The last time he had driven this route was with Mike in his own car and he had to smile when he thought of how he looked now, trundling along in the wreck. A far cry from alloys and tinted glass.

Ben's house had been a black wall, nobody home, and he was alert enough to know that turning up to the club alone might be the end of him. It was madness to go back to his own flat. He needed an ally and Mike was the safest bet. There was no way he could trust anyone else from the team, they could be wound up in the plot but he had to get to Carl. Mike was his ticket.

It was a distraught face that greeted him at the door but Curtis did not stop to ask how he was. He walked straight through the hall and up the stairs with Mike following.

"Curtis, now hold on a second, just wait."

He was in the room staring at the girl. The rigours of the day were not enough to block his appreciation of her body and he studied her. She did not flinch but stood there under his gaze for a moment before bending to the floor and throwing a top over her head. A dim recollection formed in his mind.

"Great fucking timing man. You got this one down to a second."

Mike was storming round the room in exasperation, trying to block his view of the girl as she dressed but Curtis had lost interest anyway and fell into a chair by the window. "Settle down, Mike. I think I done her before myself."

"You never sleep wid me. You see me down Maxine's, that all." She was furious at his assumption and the rage lit up her face.

"Easy, Mike. From what I hear you don't know what you a miss anyway. You have plenty of time."

Mike was struggling to believe this could be happening to him and let out a low moan. Celia was getting ready to go and he caught hold of her arm.

"Curtis, you have to go. Celia you stay. Whatever it is man, it can wait, right?"

"I afraid not."

Mike stormed across to the side of the room where Curtis sat, determined to challenge him on this. He could not rob him of Celia. But as he was about to speak he noticed the arm, hanging by the side of the chair like a dead limb. Blood was staining the outside of the bandage. He looked at his face. The skin was moist like it had been oiled and his eyes were bloodshot with fatigue. But the one aspect of his appearance that really alarmed him was his clothing. Mike had never seen him in anything damaged, dirty or old.

Curtis was known for his look. Now he sat in a filthy jacket smeared with mud and the dark stains of blood. His shirt was torn, showing part of his chest and across his lap he hugged a tatty sports bag.

"Yes, I know, me look fuck."

The girl too was examining him, paused for a second in her exit.

"You better stay, gal, we might need you. I may have people running round trying to kill me dead and I need some help."

"Well you deal with it rasta. Not my problem." She turned and opened the door, shot Mike a look that made him feel about eight years old and then rushed down the stairs. They heard the front door slam.

Mike stared on at the door until the sound of Curtis breathing heavily brought him back to life. He went over to the bed and lay back on it with a sigh. "So what do I have to do then?"

Bunny rolled his fingers on the dash. Time was moving on and they were no closer to finding their target. The massive sum that Zack had offered him rang around his head and he kept his eyes set on the doorway opposite, checking each face for Curtis. He had met him before at a meet when the youth had been driving for Carl, and Bunny never forgot a face. That was a crucial part of his business. Bunny was a side-man, a fixer, expert at stepping in and saving a situation from collapse when things had fallen apart. He was impartial. Money bought his trust and he never questioned his employer, so he had dealt with most of the players in town. Now he thought only of Curtis and the task at hand.

When he had to track a man his muscle was Alsash. He sat at the wheel of the jeep in silence. The man's sheer bulk was enough to deter most people but if it was called for, he could fight. Bunny walked behind him like infantry following a tank.

Across the street a car pulled up by the club entrance and two men jumped out of the front doors. He sat up in his seat, alert to the new arrival. A thickset man pulled himself from the rear of the car and walked quickly through the club doors. Alsash reached for his door-handle, his first movement for an hour but Bunny reached up and tapped him on the shoulder.

"It not him. That the man we have to block him see, his boss Carl. We sit and wait for our boy."

Fifteen

They were close now, only a few minutes away. Mike was driving and Curtis stared at the road, forcing his brain to think clearly about the situation. There were several things he knew had to be done before he could head for Amanda and rest. Once there he was safe, nobody could find him.

He had to assume Carl was straight on the whole thing and get the money back to him tonight. It was pushing midnight and he would be at the club by now, screaming at the team. Getting in was the main problem and that was why Mike had been recruited.

Ben would be there already and no matter what state he was in, Curtis could rely on him for help, but Mike would have to distract anyone waiting for him at the door. There was a good chance that someone would be there. They knew Carl was based at Maxine's and that was where he would head for, they also knew he was armed and that meant more shooting was a possibility. He felt for the gun by his side and thought about the way it had shaped his life in so few hours. It was a valuable friend but a dangerous one.

When they were only a few turns from the club he told Mike to pull over and they found a space and parked. Mike was quiet, but looked determined and Curtis thought back to the scene, days before, when he had wanted to establish his courage on the street. If he had wanted a testing ground then tonight would be it.

They walked briskly down the street, took a turn and came out onto a corner. Curtis hung back in the shadows but Mike stepped out and glanced at the club entrance. The crowd was thick and there were rows of cars running along the front of the club, some still trying to park. It was busy, but after some time he made out two figures sitting in an off-roader. They were motionless and this made them stand out from the other drivers who were slowly leaving their cars and joining the multitude on the pavement. He turned and went back to Curtis.

"There are two guys in a jeep. They could be waiting for you but I'm not sure. There are people all over the street, it could be anyone."

"That sound like them though, if they just sitting there."

"Yeah, could be."

"So, you know what to do, yeah?"

"Just like you said." Mike smiled at him and then walked round the corner. Despite everything, Curtis was an old friend and this was a real chance to help. He pushed his shoulders back and chest out, bracing himself for the encounter. Each stride took him nearer to the car. It hugged the shadows but he could see the man at the driver's side was immense, his head nearly touching the roof. The other had a thin face, framed by heavy dredds and Mike saw the glint of gold.

As he moved past the club door, stepping along the edge of the pavement to get around the mass of people, he saw them study his face for a second and then relax. His skin colour was not of interest. They were parked just a few cars off now and he slowed his pace. He had been aware of the noise and talk at the club door, the slam of car doors and loud greetings but now he was in a well of silence. His ears blocked out the din as he focused on the car. Reaching the passenger door he came to a halt and stared in at them but they ignored his look, concentrating on the club. He was cold with fear but failure would be worse. His hand dropped to his waist.

Bunny looked to his window at the sound. There was a thick, oily wash across the glass like pounding rain.

"Await! Man piss on the car!" He reached for the handle but paused. It would be wiser to use the other door or wait until the gush had dispersed. "Alsash, deal wid the youth!"

He was out of the car and staring over at Mike.

"Shit, sorry man. Bit drunk and didn't see you in there."

For his size the giant moved fast and Mike just managed to turn and break for the street before he reached him. Bunny stared through at his minion who was deciding if he should follow or not and cursing, but he flashed a glance down the street, suddenly thinking of the drunk as a diversion. A figure dipped past the front of the line, causing some shouts of protest from the waiting crowd and pushed through the door. It was his quarry.

He curled his lip and looked out to Alsash. "If he think I scare to go in his den then him a fool." He set his face and slipped out of the car. There may yet be a chance.

Ben had seen Carl come storming into the room, but froze in his seat. The boss man had a face like a demon at the best of times, right now he looked volcanic. Ben decided to sit it out. He had nothing to tell him anyway and he could make things worse if Curtis was pulling a move. The team bunched around a table and he watched them listening to the words of their leader intently.

The dance-floor was at capacity now. Some musicians were pacing the small stage set against the far wall, checking their equipment and waiting for the word to start the show. The singer was big in the charts at the moment and had flown in for three shows around town, sailing on a wave of publicity. People were eager to see what he was like in person. Already there was shouting and chanting from the crowd. Ben turned his attention to the stage as a flash of lights signalled his arrival. Blues and reds coloured the band, but the figure bouncing on was set in a broad spotlight of white. He was draped in a white robe and covered in gold. The metal sent yellow sparks of light shooting round the club as the spotlight caught it, like rays from the sun.

"Tell me people now, you wanna see me dance and sing?" His voice boomed across the top of the crowd, cutting out the drone from the audience. They let out a roar in response. "I say sing and dance!" It was a yell and the bass and drums kicked in behind him, laying down the beat. The crowd started to ripple, move to the sound and then caught up sync to the rhythm. As they did the keyboard cut in with a sharp melody and the unity of the band was established, whilst the DJ dropped low and started a circular grind with his hips. With no warning the music stopped dead and for an instant there was confusion in the audience but the DJ reared his head back and broke in with a growl. "Hevry gal come round, come round to me yard."

His voice rose up an octave at the end of the line and paused, then the band cut in again. This time the volume was twice as loud as before and the bass made the glass in the balcony rattle. The crowd went wild. Ben watched spellbound, wondering how it felt to be on stage.

His introspection was broken by a crash from the

entrance loud enough to be heard over the music. The team round the table rose up in one movement, eyes on the stairs. Carl remained seated.

Curtis burst into the room, every muscle taut. Ben hardly recognized his friend at first, he was so bedraggled. One arm was bandaged and hung awkwardly by his side, a bag slung across the shoulder. In his other hand he carried the gun, dirty grey metal gripped in his fist. He had come prepared for any surprises.

A space formed around him as he stared at Carl's table but he did not move. Now that he had completed his aim the strength was ebbing from his body. The side with the broken arm slumped, letting the money bag drop to the floor.

"Better take what's yours, Carl. Ash set you up bad, man."

Carl had been sizing him up, his eyes searching each strained line of Curtis's face for the truth and he was decided. His information had been correct. The youth had not been part of the cross. Now he stared at the battered sports bag, his money safe.

"Easy, Carl. I have to pick the boy up." Bunny was at the top of the stairs, standing behind Curtis. There were heavy steps behind him and Alsash strode into the room. Getting Bunny past the doormen had taken a few moments of his time.

"Is Zack who hire you in, man. Me know all about it. Now you an your man dig up, ya hear."

The tracker was not convinced. Curtis had only just walked in the room and his job was to stop contact being made. There could well have been no conversation between them and there was too much money at stake to just walk away.

"You know me independent, Carl. I have to take him. Alsash!"

The big man took a step forward and the room's occupants divided. Carl's team formed a small bunch and circled Curtis, the sports bag was scooped up and thrown onto the table in front of Carl. Those not involved shrank back against the bar and stared intently at the lone Alsash facing Carl's team.

There was a flurry of movement and he was amongst them, beating two to the floor with his first few swings. They swarmed around him, but he was impervious to the few blows they managed to land as he spun round, striking out like a cyclone. Curtis had fallen back to the seats running along the wall, his strength gone, he collapsed in exhaustion. Alsash could see his prize only yards from him and pushed onward through the defenders.

Ben had stayed at the balcony edge throughout the confrontation, but seeing Curtis helpless, he jumped off his chair and ran over to him, behind the fighters. He threw an arm around his friend and pulled him to his feet but Curtis took one step then fell back to the seats. He had blacked out. One look over his shoulder told Ben how desperate the situation was. The fight was nearly over. Like a bear patting aside the feeble assault of a pack of dogs, Alsash was striding towards him.

"You boys never learn to fight? Take a man to show you how?" Carl was on his feet at the table, his bass boom of a voice interrupting the fight. No longer did he look the elderly boss man. There was a gleam in his eye as he swept round the side of the table, tearing at his jacket and throwing it to the floor. The shades joined it. Ben saw his eyes for the first time. They were a glistening black. "Get out of my way there. Move yourself."

He pushed past the last of his team who were still in the fight and walked up to Alsash who had stopped in puzzlement. The fighter had not escaped injury altogether. His face was bleeding from the rings they wore on their fists and he was breathing heavily. Sweat ran down his neck, staining his collar and the suit he wore was ragged from tugs and pulls. But he was still powerful, far from tired and almost victorious. Carl stood between him and the target and all Alsash saw was an old man confronting him. He lurched forward, making a jab with a right fist the size of a housebrick.

With a quick dart to his left Carl was inside the sweep of the arm and reaching up with his hand. He shoved his fist into the giant's face but not as a blow. Instead, he curled his thick fingers into the mouth and jerked his arm back. There was a tearing sound like paper as Alsash felt his cheek rip open. All Carl's strength was in his chest and arms but he had enormous power there and he stepped back nimbly as blood began to stream from his adversary's wound. The bear was shocked with pain for a second but rushed forward in blind anger, doing just what Carl wished him to. Carl's fighting philosophy was that once you lost your temper then you lost the battle. He looked calm.

He locked his fingers together so the two fists became one and having done this, swept them back to his side. Just as Alsash was on him, with his long arms reaching down to Carl's throat, the linked fists rose up in a bolt of power straight into the big man's chest. The earlier punches had little effect on him but this was different. Carl had focused all his strength into the blow and rammed it home with a fierce yell, driving it deep into the body. Alsash fell in a heap, winded, but Carl showed no mercy. He stepped over to the kneeling wreck and kicked him in the side of the head with the heel of his shoe, neatly finishing the job.

"Sometimes it pay to fight dirty, you hear me."

Sixteen

There were voices just beyond the door and at first he thought he was still dreaming, stuck in the nightmare of the stone corridor with Ash bleeding at his feet, but the shape of the room began to clear and he noticed the familiar debris lying on the floor. This was his bedroom.

Sitting up in the bed, he saw his reflection in a desk mirror on the far wall and examined his features, relieved that he was not as bruised as he felt. His hand was neatly bandaged and the pain was only slight, but the memory of the injury flooded back and he lay down again, closing his eyes. After a moment he pushed the covers off the bed and swung his legs onto the floor. There was no point dwelling on the loss, after all he was no artist or piano player, he could get by.

Getting to his feet was an experience. A burst of nausea and dizziness in his head almost made him sink back to the bed but after a few seconds it cleared and he walked over to his wardrobe, intent on dressing.

"Where you off to? Get back into bed right now." Ben strode into the room with an authoritative air. He was smartly dressed in a style suit, carrying a brown paper bag, stuffed with groceries. Curtis stared at him.

"That's my suit you're wearing. Who said you could raid my wardrobe then?"

There were steps behind Ben's dapper body and Mike appeared. "Await, you too?"

Mike was in similar dress, white shirt and black jacket and trousers. Both of them looked like kids caught shoplifting.

"Didn't think you'd mind man, you being laid out an' that. Never had a chance to check your wardrobe before."

They were shuffling from foot to foot, exchanging nervous glances. Curtis broke into a smile.

"It alright. You look pretty sharp as it is. Now you can help me choose something."

He moved back to the clothes on the rail but Ben stepped forward, laying his shopping on the bed. "Oh no. You not going anywhere. You gonna rest up, right here."

"That's right C. Doctor's orders."

"No, sah. I have things to do. Have a girl to see."

"Oh, I spoke with her yesterday." Ben was acting all casual, as though he had the upper hand now. He sat on the corner of the bed, idly looking at the instructions on a tin of soup he had taken from the bag.

"What you mean, yesterday? You dep on the club after you talk with her and not tell me?" He was finding his strength now and the anger showed on his face but Ben and Mike started to chuckle. "This aint funny you fuckers. Where is she?" He rushed to Ben and grabbed him hard at the elbow.

"Watch it, Curtis. You mess up your suit here."

They were laughing out loud now and Curtis stared at them both in amazement. "So, why you not tell me? Did she sound angry or something?"

"Curtis in love I think, Mikey."

"Ben, talk you . . ."

"The reason I said nothing is cause you been asleep, my friend." He stood up and walked over to Curtis, slapping him on the shoulder. "You been asleep for two days straight. Not a sound come out of you. Carl have someone look over you, fix you up. Then he gave we some dollar and tell us look after you. When you up you is to go see him."

"Two day? Two day I sleep?"

"Like a baby. Now, how you want your soup?"

"Fuck the soup. Me ring her now."

He was dazed at the length of time that had passed. Things needed to be attended to and he rushed about the room trying to dress. His two companions watched, smiling.

"So what the big joke then?"

"Everything set man. We having a drink-up for you down at Bliss tonight, so you see her then."

He fell back onto the bed with a sigh.

"So anything else you sort out when I snoozing, Ben?"

"Well, I tell her to bring a friend for me."

The drive to the club was slow but Curtis settled down in the comfort of his car and took in the passing scenery. It was late afternoon and the streets were packed with traffic but instead of the backstreet cuts he would usually take he sat it out on the highroad, crawling in the traffic. The shops and faces of West Park were a welcome and reassuring sight.

It was the last light of day when he pulled up at the club. The street was empty compared with the rush of a club-night, almost ghostly.

In the daytime Maxine's was more of a den for the team than a Club. After ringing the bell for a few minutes one of the guys came down to let him in, yawning but giving him a warm greeting. Curtis felt the change as he followed him up to the top room. A small group of them sat round a table, drinking coffee and chatting but his arrival brought a warm response, not like the times before when he was more of an apprentice, the youngster. He had earned respect now and each one of them looked upon him as an equal. By now they had all heard the tale of the gunplay.

"Where Carl then?"

"Round the back of the bar, man."

He left them at the table and walked through to the

bar area, going through to the small store-room that Carl used as an office. Past the empty crates and boxes he saw the boss at his small table. This was the way he got paid and Curtis almost felt offended. After going through that ordeal and being straight with Carl he was still just the office boy, being called in to collect his wage and a slap on the back.

"So, Curtis, you show. Well how you feel, sah?" Carl stood up from his seat and stuck a fat fist out in the air.

Curtis noted the gesture and returned his for the contact. Never before had Carl given him this symbol of union.

"Now, park youself up and tek this, afore I forget." He handed him the standard envelope from a pile on the table. "Gwan. Open it up and count, man. Only a fool don't count his money."

He tore the seal, holding the base of it against his chest with the bandaged hand. Looking up he saw Carl studying the motion and he suddenly became insecure at his handicap. "It heal up fast man. Just a bit tender."

"Sure, sure."

He was about to speak again, to argue his case but he had the paper torn now and his eyes studied the contents. The envelope had been thin, but instead of the usual clutch of tens and twenties he saw the magical, green glimmer of fifties. They were mint and so lay flat against one another and he had to separate them slowly. Carl broke in by the time he got to twenty.

"There is the same number as is written on the note my friend. You get a bonus, C."

He kept flicking through them but not counting anymore. The money felt good to touch.

"So, you help me, I help you. But I was confused fo' a while man. See, by the time you get here I may have been in a bad mood wid you, but I hear talk you know."

Curtis looked up from the money. Carl was staring at him intently.

"Only one thing make sure you is on my side."

Now his face was relaxed. He had secured his attention and was drawing out the suspense.

"Man come see me, tell me you is bad right through and for a while I believe him. Only one thing is telling me you straight. You wanna know?"

Curtis was lost. He had assumed that him coming back with the money was his testimony. He must tell him what Ash had said. "But when I reach, you know I was with you, Carl, that it."

"No, sah. Me would a kill you dead if that had been all. No, me have a little friend who help me from time to time."

He paused for a moment and Curtis sensed what he was doing. His words had not shocked Curtis, they were part of the normal stance. He was putting himself on top again, proving he was still the man, in the same way he had with Alsash. Ben had told him of the fight. Carl did not want any one of the team thinking he was not in control.

He turned and rapped on the door behind him. "Marian, you come now."

The bare, plywood door creaked open and she came through in answer to his call, sliding round behind him and curling a hand to the back of his head. Hair fell across the curve in her neck and down to a loose blouse. In these drab surroundings her beauty was an alien light and it took him a few seconds to move his eyes from her face.

"This one of my girls, C. She lie with that fucker Zack from time to time, at my instruction. That so, Marian?"

The girl hugged her mentor and dropped her lips to his ear, blowing a soft kiss to his cheek. All the time she stared at Curtis, noting his expression. "I'm your eyes and ears baby."

"You see, C? I have a finger on the breath a the town. She tell me Ash round there and things make sense." His huge chest heaved with laughter and the girl giggled as if by command.

"So where Zack then? You have him?"

"No, him dig up. He have problem with the man he pair with. But Zack get round it, him slippy man. Now, you dig up sah and not worry 'bout him."

Curtis stuffed the envelope in his jacket and pushed his chair back to leave.

"Remember C., Carl not forget what you done. Bell me later, yeah?" He made for the door then turned back to whisper thanks for the reward. Carl and the girl were kissing, like father and daughter.

Mike slammed the tray down on the wood, spilling the drinks so the liquid spread across the wood in a black stain.

"Easy man, you drunk already?"

"Ah, this break me. You should be grateful."

"Don't worry yourself. I thank you kindly."

Ben smiled at him from the corner of the booth. He was squashed in next to the wall by Curtis and playfully nudged along the bench.

"Yes Ben, you need some air?"

"Think is the girl who need air, man."

Amanda was on the end. Curtis had his arm draped over her shoulder and she was flushed from his kisses.

"So, me not see her for a while, you know."

"Excuse me, I have a name you know."

Ben and Mike started laughing as Curtis turned back to her and muttered an apology at her shoulder.

The bar was in the early lift of the evening, people starting to stream in for the coming night.

"So, Mike, you say you broke?"

"Yeah, kind of." He was dipping his face to the table, ashamed that he had run out of money with the first round. This was supposed to be a party for his friend's safe return and he felt guilty not being able to treat him to a few drinks. Ben was bust too, but as usual he was relaxed about it.

"Well, stick this behind the bar then."

Curtis reached over and forced a note into his hand. It was one of the fifties Carl had given him. "Don't want to go short, anyway is me who should be buying everyone drinks. Was you who help me out, remember?"

He was directing his eyes at Mike and his friend blushed, then walked over to the bar.

"So what now C? You carry on with Carl?"

"For a bit longer, yeah."

"We're going away for a while, Ben." Amanda had leant forward and delivered the words with a sarcastic twist. Then she turned back to Curtis with an inquisitive stare.

"Well, if I can get the time off, yeah."

"So, you had better keep a hand on that generosity of yours, wouldn't you agree?"

There was a noise at the bar and Curtis was glad at the distraction. Mike was being hassled by a rather portly, middle-aged man. He was tugging at his arm as Mike walked back to the table.

"Look. I really have no idea what you're talking about."

"Don't give me that. It was you. I'm not alone, you know." He stopped in the centre of the room and called back to his table. "Lads! This is one of the bastards that did me a few nights ago."

There was a shuffle and he was joined by three, stout men of about the same age. They were all dressed in smart casuals and had probably been to work before breaking for a drink.

Mike had come over to the table and sat down. "I don't know why he's so riled. Never seen him before."

"Oh yes you have." Ben was moving off the seat. He kept his eyes on the advancing men but started to edge towards the rear door.

Curtis looked around him, perplexed. "Mike, Ben, wha go on?"

The man who had started the shouting was at the table now, his face red with anger. "And that's the other one."

He pointed at Ben.

"What's he on about?" Mike was confused by the situation and turned to Ben for the answer.

"It's the guy we rolled, innit?"

Curtis rolled his head back and let out a howl of laughter as Ben jumped from the seat. There was just room for the two friends to squeeze past their accusers and break for the street but the men followed them out to give chase. Curtis and Amanda could see the pursuit through the long, glass window by the bench.

"You not going to help them?"

"Oh, they fine. Ben and Mike can get away no problem. They still youth." He lifted his glass and took a sip, lost in thought for a moment. The last few days had seen his ascent in the team and Amanda was by his side now. Everything had worked out. There was time for a trip away with her and then he could return and enjoy his new status. Ben and Mike still had some growing up to do but he knew where he was going now, he had stepped into manhood.

"Come now. Let's spend some more of that money at the bar. I think the boys may be gone some time."

JONATHAN BROOK is twenty-six years old and was born in Los Angeles, California. At 6 years old his family relocated to Leeds, Yorkshire where he was soon installed in the local comprehensive and did nothing of particular note except learn how to play the guitar and skank. As a member of an almost-known Ska outfit he toured the UK for a number of years, finding time to write reviews and music articles along the way. Moving to London in the late Eighties Jonathan did more of the same including studio work and US/Japanese tours for many an Acid Jazz band including The Night Trains and the Humble Souls. The closest he has ever come to any sort of stability has been his last three years' work with rocksteady superhero Desmond Dekker. SLACKNESS is his first novel.

Also in the *Backstreets* series

BIG UP!

With Curtis now reaping the rewards of his increasingly dangerous gangster lifestyle, it's up to Ben and Mike to make their own runnings—with Curtis' help of course.

Taking their reputations in their hands the lads venture into the world of club promotions and to their relish find everything they could want—sex and drugs and ragga too! But the fun and games can only last so long. Someone out there obviously doesn't like them—or their success . . .

BIG UP! the second BACKSTREETS novel continues the action first introduced in SLACKNESS, also available from Boxtree.